Murky Waters Rising

Vanity Smith

DEDICATION

This one is for you, Chasity! You are loved beyond words and missed beyond measure.

ACKNOWLEDGMENTS

To my partner, lover and friend, none of this would have been possible without your contributions, patience, and support. I love you. To my friends and family that helped me along the way, thank you. I appreciate you more than you'll ever know.

PROLOGUE
JEN

MLK WEEKEND 2003

I was getting ready to leave Sasha's when Lace insisted on staying over with me. We packed the kids up, and Nika packed up DD, and we all left Sasha's at the same time. I tried calling Axel on the way in to see if he needed anything while I was out, but he didn't answer. I pulled into my parking spot, and Lace pulled in right next to me. I was ready to get into the house and hang with my man for a bit. I really wished Lace had stayed at Sasha's. I wanted alone time with Axel.

"Hold on!" Lace yelled as I was about to enter the house.

"Can you give me a hand?" she asked. I walked back over to her car and grabbed T's bag. Her hands weren't full; she didn't need the help. We walked to the door laughing about a story Sasha shared with us earlier that day. I opened the door and walked in. I heard Lace scream before I saw anything.

"Alisha, T," she yelled, "come with me!" she said as she ushered the kids out the house. I stood there in disbelief. Axel was laid out on the floor. I ran over to Axel and attempted CPR, but it was too late. He was gone. I could tell he was dead by the dried-up foam that had come out of his mouth, and he had no pulse. I don't remember screaming any, but I do remember crying and crying hysterically. Lace called 911 and must have called Nika and Sasha right after. They arrived within minutes of the cops arriving.

"""

CHAPTER 1
LACE

#Spring 2003

It was bittersweet as I packed up my blue Dodge Durango. It was a beautiful spring day in 2003, perfect for a drive to Florida. The weather report called for several thunderstorms, but the sky was clear, and the sun was shining—the calm before the storm.

My tour was over in Maryland, and now it was time to move on. Over the next two days, I would be making the drive from Maryland to Miami, Florida, and then from Miami to Pensacola. My destination, however, was Norfolk, VA. I had been accepted into an advanced specialty school in Pensacola, where I would spend the summer in training. It was going to be a challenging road trip with my 3-year-old son, Terrance, whose nickname is T, in tow. I asked Nathan, my brother, to help with the drive, and he flew in from St. Louis a few nights early to help me pack up.

Nathan and I were the two closet siblings. My parents had four children. Simba was the oldest, then Nathan, followed by me and my younger sister, Yanni. Nathan and I talked every day, even though he lived in St Louis and I in Maryland.

Our parents were married for 32 years and very much in love. Growing up, there were many days my dad would walk up behind my mother while she was washing dishes or cooking, and kiss her on the neck, and whisper something that made her giggle like a little schoolgirl on the playground. It was probably some old nasty freaky shit. They were sick in love. Mom would sit on Dad's lap and tell him about her day, and he would listen intently, holding her hand, or fondling her hair. This was their daily routine.

Sometimes during dinner, Mom would reach out her hand, and Dad would grab it, and they would hold hands while they ate silently. It was as if she knew he wouldn't always be around, so she touched him as often as she could. Dad was the same as her. She could never simply walk past him without him feeling her up, and she loved it.

Dad passed a few years ago, and it's been hard on everyone, especially me. I am a true daddy's girl. I loved my father, and he loved me, and everyone knew it. I was his favorite. My father loved the others just the same, but it was no secret that he had a special love for me, and he never tried to hide it. I was purposely planned, wanted, and adored. He showered me with love and attention.

"It's your personality, ambition, and energy that I like about you, Lacey Michelle," Dad once said. "You're so young, yet so intelligent and mature. It blows me away sometimes. You know you get that all from me," he said with a chuckle.

"You're my real twin."

My father had a twin brother, but he always joked about me being his real twin. Surprisingly, we looked nothing alike. My father was a muscular man that stood 6'4 and was very dark-skinned. I'm slim with curves in all the right places. I'm almost 5'5, and with a good tan, my complexion is dark caramel. Without a tan, I'm almost ghostly looking.

My eyes are slightly slanted, and my nose is small and girly like. My father, on the other hand, had beautiful, big, brown, round eyes and a thick masculine nose that sloped toward the nostrils. I guess you could say we did have the same lips. They were thick and luscious.

My father treated me like his twin too. We did everything and went everywhere together. If you saw him, you saw me. I think he did that by design. When I was in high school, I couldn't even skip school without someone asking, "Aren't you Brownie's daughter? Why aren't you in school? Let me give him a call and see if he knows you're on this side of town." Random people would say. After the third time of being snitched on, I stopped skipping school. It just wasn't worth the trouble. Plus, I enjoyed school. I was in a cosmetology program, which was three of my classes every day. It was a three-year program that taught the basics of cosmetology, which included hair, nails, wax, massage, etc. I was one of the best students.

After my high school graduation, I took my state boards and passed on the first try. I was so proud, as were my parents. I quickly landed a job at a prestigious hair salon in Miramar. I did hair in the salon for two years. It was great in the beginning, but gradually, it became overwhelming. My clients loved me and would wait for hours to sit in my chair. They scheduled appointments months in advance to guarantee their time slot. Business was good!

I lived at home with my parents and was able to pocket all my cash. I hadn't planned on moving out of my parents' house until I married my high school sweetheart, and we purchased a home of our own.

I was so in love with my boyfriend that every decision I made was decided with him in mind. I wanted what my parents had and thought I had found that with my boyfriend. I was blissfully in love, living my life. Working in the salon, building my clientele and popularity, while he was off having babies with another woman.

I can talk about it now, but it was devastating back then. I lost my virginity

to this fool, and he was out sowing his wild oats while I was preparing for our future. I was so naïve. After his first child was born, I knew I needed to leave. I couldn't be in the same place as him without being with him.

But my father had just fallen ill, and I wanted to be close to him. I was torn trying to make the best decision for me and my heart. I loved my father and wanted to be close, just in case he needed me. But I hated my boyfriend – because he was, in fact, still my boyfriend until the third child was born – and I could no longer stomach the sight of him.

Things started to shift for me. Seeing my father sick was heartbreaking all over again as if my heart hadn't just been broken. My father was the strongest man I knew, and to see him so weak was crushing.

I started losing interest in doing hair. Working 7 days a week, no days off from 7a.m. – 11 p.m., was demanding. Yea, the money was good, but I was getting over it fast. I devoted so much time to work, using it as a distraction from the pain I was enduring, that I became dissatisfied. I felt like my life was in an upheaval. I was miserable. I was losing the love of my life twice.

I needed something different but didn't quite know what it was. On one Wednesday, I called out sick to try and wrap my brain around the shift my life was taking. I stayed in bed most of the day but decided to join the family for dinner. Mom had made one of Dad's favorite meals. After we had eaten, my parents sat on the sofa extremely close to each other, because there was no way they would ever sit apart. I sat in the oversized chair to the right and watched them, Yanni sat across from me in the love seat. Mom rested her head on Dad's chest as they watched jeopardy and got every answer wrong. He whispered something to her, and she began to giggle like she always did. My eyes began to water; I sensed that my father saw me. I hadn't told them about what was going on with my boyfriend and me; I still hoped that things would work out. But the state of our relationship being what it was, I knew deep inside that there would never be a future for us.

"What's wrong, Lacey Michelle?" Dad always called me by my full name. Lace was never good enough for him.

"I don't know!" I responded. Of course, I knew, but Yanni was sitting in the living room with us, and I didn't want to talk in front of her. I looked at Yanni, and Mom knew my feelings.

"Yanni, can you excuse us while we talk to Lace?" Yanni, with her stank attitude, got up and walked out. She was born that way. Always mad at the world.

Once Yanni was out of sight, I tried as best I could to explain everything that was happening and how I was feeling while also trying to make sense. I failed miserably. Mom finally spoke and asked, "Are you happy here, Lace?"

"No."

Dad leaned toward me and simply said, "Your mom and I are happy because we always choose us. No one else matters. We always choose us first. Lacey Michelle, you are at that age where you must choose you first if you want to be happy. I'm sick, not dead. Don't worry about me, or Mom, or anyone else! Go be happy, whatever that means for you."

That was it. That was all my loving parents had to offer me. They sat back on the sofa and continued getting all the wrong answers, this time to Wheel of Fortune. I replayed my dad's words for the next few days. The problem was that I didn't know what would make me happy. I just knew I needed something different and far away from Miami. A few days later, I walked into a Navy recruiting station wearing a short pair of cut-off shorts and a white tank top and no bra. I jokingly asked, "Are y'all hiring?"

Both recruiters laughed. "We're always hiring, come in and have a seat." That was in May. I shipped out in October of 1998.

####

Children weren't allowed at military training facilities, so Nathan and I were heading for Miami first to drop T off. My mother and T's father agreed to care for him while I completed training, which was a short three months, and basically their shared summertime visitation. We were just about finished packing the truck when Mrs. Thompson strolled over. "You will be missed, Lace," Mrs. Thompson said as she threw her arms around me. I hugged her long and tight.

Mrs. Thompson was my neighbor to the right of me in a row of townhomes in Spring Meadows. Mrs. Thompson and I didn't get along initially because she was so damn nosey and mean. She stayed in my business and my damn parking spot! That was the real problem. After months of back and forth tension, I finally gave up and let her have the parking spot.

Nathan was still in the house, gathering the final items to pack into the truck. He walked out of the house with an arm full of boxes just as we ended our embrace. He tipped his head to the side and giggled as he walked up. He knew our past and was shocked that the two of us were able to get past all the dissension that once fueled our existence. "I'll miss you too, Mrs. Thompson." T was wrapped around Mrs. Thompson's legs at this point, not wanting to let go.

I remember the day our relationship changed. It was shortly after I had arrived in the winter of 2001. I had been so sick I couldn't get out of bed. I fell ill on Friday. Sunday came around, and I still hadn't left the house. That was very unusual for me, and Mrs. Thompson knew I lived for the weekends. Happy hour was for sure on the list every Friday night. I would wake up early on Saturdays and take T to one of his many playdates. If there was nothing planned, T and I would usually hit DC and spend the day at one of the free museums. T loved that type of stuff. He wanted to learn everything he could about everything he saw. T kept me on my toes. We often learned things together.

Saturday nights were dedicated to my sex life. I would hit the DC nightlife with friends from work. Sundays were usually for recovery and dinner with T and friends. I entertained like crazy too. If it wasn't associates from work, it was a random ass guy that was sexy and interesting enough to fuck, but I only entertained men after 8:30 p.m., which was T's bedtime. Even on weekends, I maintained a strict bedtime. I read an article once that said kids of T's age need about 10-13 hours of sleep. I was committed to making sure T had all the sleep he needed. Some of the reasons might have been a bit selfish; nevertheless, he was always well-rested.

I was lying on the sofa where I had been since Friday night. And there was a knock on my door. No one had called, so I assumed it was no one important. After I didn't answer, they knocked again and again. The knocking became so persistent that it forced me to move off the sofa. I lumbered to the door, using all the strength I had. I opened the door, and there stood Mrs. Thompson. I didn't even have the energy to speak. I just let the door swing open and walked back to the sofa.

Mrs. Thompson walked in and looked around. After taking note of what seemed like every inch of my kitchen and living room, she finally spoke, in her southerly scratching tone: "What's wrong with you, girl? Is it fever, body aches cramps, or what?"

"I think it's all the above. I'm not sure," I replied. Mrs. Thompson walked over and put her hand on my forehead. T had then crawled up close to me.

"Child, you're burning up." Mrs. Thompson stepped back for a second, looked around again, and started walking toward the door. "I'll be right back!" she said as she disappeared through the door. I lay there and didn't even think about her ole nosey ass again. I knew in my heart she was just there to pry, and I was so thankful my house was in decent order… "Ole hag!" I thought silently.

I woke up to the slight smell of something pervading throughout the house, I reached for T, but he was no longer clinched to my side. "T," I yelled.

Mrs. Thompson peered her head out of the kitchen and said, "He's in here with me."

"What are you doing here?" I asked.

"I came back with some chicken noodle soup and medicine, but you were fast asleep. I fed T and cleaned up the dishes for you. I have also made a few other things, so you can eat to nourish your body back to health," she said as she put her head back in the kitchen and continued doing whatever she was doing.

Seconds later, she appeared again walking into the living room with a piping hot bowl of chicken soup. Here I was, thinking Mrs. Thompson was just a nosey hag, and to my surprise, she genuinely cared about me, my son, and my health.

I saw Mrs. Thompson differently after that day. Being so far away from my own mother and family, she became the family I needed. Many nights I worked late, she would pick T up from daycare, feed him, help him with his reading and writing skills, bathe him, read him bedtime stories, and stay over until I made it home. She was like a second mother to me. She protected me as only a mother would.

"Everything is packed, and we're ready to go," Nathan announced.

"Cool, let me give it one last walkthrough, and we can head out." I walked through my small townhouse one last time and remembered all the good times had. I managed to shove the memories of the murder that took place in the house to the back of my mind. That was one reason I chose to rent the townhouse out instead of selling it. I couldn't take the chance of a home inspection or selling it to someone that wanted to do any work. I had to preserve the place. I walked out and closed and locked the door behind me. "Goodbye, Maryland! Good ridings, Sargent Carlos Hendricks, you piece of shit rapist asshole!" I mumbled softly. Nathan hopped in the driver seat as I strapped T in. I waved goodbye to my good neighbor as I climbed into the passenger seat. I put on my seat belt, looked at Nathan, and smiled. "I'm ready, brother; let's hit it!"

As Nathan drove, I sat watching the cars as we passed them by. It was a long 21-hour drive, but with the way Nathan was driving, I was for sure we would make it in 17 hours. The ride allowed me way too much time to reminisce. Flashbacks of the murders I participated in tried to creep into my thoughts, but I dismissed them instantly every time.

Professionally, work was good for me in Maryland. I advanced from E-3 to E-5 in just 18 months. My job was exciting, and I learned a tremendous amount.

Personally, I had become someone I wasn't sure I liked, or maybe I did like who I had become. Maybe I liked her a little too much and felt guilty about it. The growth and acceptance of who I had become showed in my social life, which had become erratic and exotic. I purposely didn't emotionally connect with anyone during my time in Maryland. I made a few friends that I would cherish for sure, but none like the friends I had in VA. I kept my distance from anything that looked like it could become a love interest. After two major heartbreaks in six years, I was not interested in finding love. I was still trying to get over Marcus, my second heartbreak.

CHAPTER 2

#Spring 2001: Pensacola

It was my first time in Pensacola. I was there to complete my entry-level training, also known as A-school. By this time, I had been in the Navy for almost three years. My first tour was at a squadron in Virginia, where I met Nika, Sasha, and Jen.

Since I had already been to the fleet, I was listed as a fleet returnee. As I was checking in, I was directed to a 10-story building that looked very similar to a three or four-star hotel. There was a lavish grey sign with white trim that stood on the lawn that read, Dorsey Hall, in bold black letters.

When I entered the building, I noticed that the lobby was sleek and inviting. I walked up to the front desk and gave the young lady a copy of my orders. "Welcome to Naval Technical Training Center, Corey Station Pensacola," the young lady spoke in an exciting tone as she checked me into my room. I studied the area while the young lady performed her duties. When she spoke again, her voice startled me: "Airman Miles, here is your informational packet and your keys. The bellhop will assist you with your things," she had said. I was then escorted to my room, 402 A, by the bellhop. The bellhop offered some instructions and a quick tour of my suite, making sure to point out the common areas of my living quarters.

This was all completely new to me. Apparently, this is how you're treated after you've done a tour in the fleet. "Concierge services and bellhops!" I smiled at the thought. I made several trips up and down the elevator, collecting the rest of my things from the truck. Strangely, I still hadn't seen much activity. After a couple of hours, I was exhausted and hungry. I read over the material, as instructed, and realized I was much too tired to eat. I prepared my uniform for the next day, showered, and called it a night. I was excited about my new possibilities. I couldn't wait to start and finish this training.

The next morning, referencing the instructional packet I received from yesterday, I proceeded to the convocation center. I walked in about 07:31. The center was completely packed. I was amongst a few stragglers walking in. From the looks of it, everyone else had a different reporting time. There were no available seats, so I stood against the back wall near the entry. Orientation was long and boring as to
be expected. Fleet returnees were given the option of going on a campus

tour or taking the rest of the day off. I chuckled within me. I'll always take the off day.

I did want to find the galley, though. I was starving. I saw a few individuals walking out once the fleet returnees were dismissed. I stood and watched them for a minute or so to see the direction they were headed. As I stood there, I felt a tap on my shoulder. I turned around and looked into the face of a gorgeous, tall black man.

He stood about 6'3 with an athletic build. He wore the uniform of the day with a crisp white-t. He smiled, "Hey, Lace! It's me, Marcus!"

I returned the smile, though I was a little confused. "Nice to meet you, Marcus."

"Nice to meet me? You can't be serious, Lace! You don't remember me? I know who you are," he continued.

"Yea, OK!" I kind of rolled my eyes. I would never forget a face like his, so I knew he must have been mistaken. "Do you know where the galley is?" I asked.

"Sure, I was heading there myself. We'll eat together; it will give us time to talk and catch up," Marcus said. "Talking is the last thing I want to do with this man," I thought.

The galley was very different from what I remembered also. We found a table near the back. Shortly after sitting, someone came over to take our orders. I was so confused. Apparently, there was a galley for fleet returnees and a different galley for newcomers. The newcomers', also known as Booters, meaning straight out of boot camp, galley was what I remembered; standing in long lines for cold-ass eggs and stale bread. This galley was different. Everything was made to order.

I ordered a farmer's omelet with toast and a short stack. Marcus looked at me in disbelief and ordered the exact same meal. "You are not going to eat all that food?" he said.

"Watch me!" I replied. We both laughed.

Our food came much faster than expected. Marcus talked to me like we had been friends for years as we ate. I was so puzzled but too embarrassed to ask where we knew each other from. "Could he have been a VA random? I think I would have remembered him if he was," I thought to myself. Marcus continued to talk throughout the meal as I listened attentively, trying to place how I knew him. We finished breakfast and began heading back toward my building.

"Where are you staying?" Marcus asked.

"Dorsey Hall," I replied casually. With genuine excitement, Marcus spoke through his super-wide smile,

"So am I! What room are you in, Lace?"

I chuckled, not really knowing what to think of all this. "I am in room 402A."

Marcus stopped and stood still directly in front of me; "I am in room 402B," he said through a smile bigger than the last.

"This must be a joke. The suites can't be unisex," I said as I waved him off and walked away.

"Well, it looks like they are," Marcus insisted, following close behind me.

We both entered Dorsey Hall, looking at each other strangely. We walked over to the elevator, and I pushed the button to go up. I entered the elevator, as did Marcus. "Are you going to hit the button for your floor?" I asked.

Marcus smiled at me with his gorgeous white teeth and pushed the number four. I became anxious, and my blood heated up on the inside. I busted out laughing and couldn't stop. "That sometimes happens when I get anxious. This has got to be a joke." I walked into my suite, and Marcus walked in behind me. I went to my door, and he went to 402B.

I put my key in, and he fell out laughing, "Got ya! Did you really think they would put us in the same suite? Qui said I could get you! I had you thinking we knew each other too, didn't I?"

I stood there. Plotting… "Who the fuck are you, asshole?"

Marcus continued laughing, a good hearty gut-busting laugh. He was so tickled. After what seemed like an eternity of him laughing, he was finally able to speak. "My name really is Marcus. I was stationed with Qui, in Norfolk. I'm in room 401A."

Qui is a good friend of mine. We hung out often. I wonder why he had never brought Marcus around. "Why haven't I met you if you and Qui are friends?" I asked.

"I'm not sure. It just wasn't meant for us to meet in Norfolk, I guess. Qui did make me promise to keep an eye on you. We're neighbors," Marcus proudly announced. "Since we have the day off, do you want to go to the beach? I've never been," Marcus continued.

"Is this your first time in Pensacola?" I asked.

"Yes, but I meant I had never been to any beach," he replied nonchalantly.

I looked at him in disgust. "You are such a liar. Who has never been to a beach?" I asked.

"I haven't. I was born and raised in the District of Columbia, and before joining the Navy, I had never left south-east."

"*Wow!*" I thought silently to myself in disbelief, but because I love the beach, why not have a beach day.

I conceded to Marcus' request. "Give me some time to get ready, and then we can head out." I hadn't really unpacked, but being a Miami girl, I had so many bathing suits; it shouldn't be hard to find one. After going through several bags, I finally found my turquoise string bikini bottom. I wasn't sure if it was a string bikini kind of day, so I kept digging. I pulled out a few other items, including the halter-top to the bikini bottom. I dug for a few more minutes and came up empty. "String bikini day, it is!" I took off my uniform and placed it on the hanger in the closet. I slipped my panties off and slipped my bikini bottom on.

As I was taking off my bra, I could feel someone staring at me. I turned my head to the left to look behind me, and lo and behold, Marcus was standing in the doorway watching me undress. I almost hid myself, but the devil in me took over. I turned and faced Marcus, so he could see me. I removed my bra and allowed him to see my perfect breast fall out. I threw my bra on the bed and pulled my halter top on, smiled, and turned away from him. I bent over to show my ass in my string bikini instead of kneeling down to gather the rest of the items I needed for the beach out of my bag. As I was bending over, I felt something strong and hard against my ass. I smiled and didn't even acknowledge it. I continued to gather my things, throwing them in the closest tote bag I could find. He watched me carefully. "I'm ready," I announced as I stood up straight, still with my back toward him. I felt his breath. He was breathing heavily. I poked my ass out and pushed him softly away from me. "Are you ready?" I asked, looking him in the eye.

"In more ways than one," he replied.

I giggled at the sight of his dick bulging through his shorts. I placed my hand on his cock and pushed him slightly out of my way. My insides became warm; he was surely blessed.

The beach was a cool twenty-minute ride. We talked the entire time. I was amazed at how much we had in common, and the chemistry was crazy between us. It was a postcard-ready beach day. The sun shone bright, and the breeze was perfect. We found a nice spot in the sand. I started going through my tote, pulling out all sorts of beach goodies. I grabbed a blanket, shook it out, and placed it in the sand. I pulled out my beach pillow and sunscreen as well. We settled on our blanket and talked a little longer while I slathered myself with sunscreen. When I was done, I was ready to hit the water.

Although Marcus had never been to a beach, he was a keen swimmer. We swam and played in the water like teenagers. We talked for hours. When the sun started to set, I began to pack up, and Marcus decided to go for one last swim. His body moved flawlessly through the ocean. He finished his swim and began walking toward me. The rays of the sun hit him in all the right places; the water glistened across his body; he was the image of an African God, his body carved to perfection. His swim trunks clung to his wet body, and I could see the imprint of my new favorite toy. It was at that moment that I decided I would make him mine.

The connection between us was much too strong for Marcus to be a random—you know—a random guy whose name you wouldn't care to remember. I felt like I wanted something more with him. This was the first time I wanted more than just a fuck since my first heartbreak. Marcus and I became inseparable. I was surely falling for him, and I wanted him to be mine. There was only one problem—Marcus had a girlfriend and a son back home waiting for him. My father raised me to know my worth; I had already been played the fool once, and I wasn't ready to be played again. I wanted to be Marcus' one and only, and I surely wouldn't play second to someone's baby mama.

Despite knowing all of this I still wanted Marcus badly. I found myself wondering if I should just enjoy the time with Marcus and attempt convincing myself that he was a random with a purpose. Maybe I could train my mind to believe that. My feelings for Marcus became overwhelming, as did my sexual desire for him. We lived right next door, and the walls were super thin. As soon as one alarm clock went off, we were both up. We did everything together, and I needed a break.

We met up every morning for muster while we waited to class up. Every day, we were assigned an arbitrary job. Some days, we would get lucky and not be given any assignment. Those were the hardest days for me. It seemed like we always got the same assignment and the same days off. This made it difficult for me to avoid him, but I had to find a way. I found myself leaving muster just a little bit early or staying behind to talk to someone just to avoid walking and talking to Marcus. I made it a routine.

In my second week of this, Marcus caught on. One day, after noon, I got back to my room, after lingering around the muster area for far too long, and found Marcus sitting outside my door.

"Lace, we need to talk," Marcus said sternly as he stood up. I opened the suite door and walked in. Marcus followed closely behind.

"What's up?" I asked as I sat on the bed.

"Why have you been avoiding me, Lace?" Marcus asked as he stood guard at the door, ensuring I didn't make a run for it, I assumed.

"I'm not avoiding you; I've just been busy. That's all!"

Truth is, him standing in front of me demanding answers made me want him even more. I wanted more than to just fuck him, though. I wanted to love him. I wanted to be one with him. I wanted him in me, running through my blood. "No, Lace, you haven't been busy. You've been avoiding me. Tell me what's up. I thought we were friends," Marcus said, interrupting my thoughts.

"We are friends. I just needed a friendship break. That's all!" I replied.

"What the fuck is a friendship break?" Marcus snarled.

"You wouldn't understand," I responded with a deep eye-roll.

"How do you know what I would understand? Give me the benefit of the doubt, why don't you? Explain it to me, Lace," Marcus demanded.

"I just needed some quality Lace-time," I sighed.

Marcus finally moved away from the door and sat in the recliner. "Well, if you need Lace-time, I get and respect that, but I need Lace-time too. We're an item. You can't just cut me out like that," Marcus said in a soft sweet tone.

I laughed. "An item? Sir, you have an entire girlfriend back home."

Marcus looked at me with the most serious look I had ever seen on his face, and spoke sternly yet again, "Yea, I do! But you know how I feel about her. We have a kid together, that's all."

I don't know why, but I was near tears, trying hard to hold it together through my words, "Marcus, I want more than a friendship, and I know that's unattainable with you. It's hard for me to continue the friendship, just as friends. Sometimes, I'm going to have to take friendship breaks. That's all there is to it." Marcus moved from the recliner and sat next to me on the bed.

He grabbed my hand and spoke softly, but condescendingly, "I classed up today, while you were on your friendship break. Do you know what that means, Lace?"

I responded in the same sweet condescending tone, "Yes, you start class next week."

Marcus didn't like my tone. He wasn't used to being challenged by anyone, especially not a woman.

He softened his tone, "Well yea, Lace, that too, but more importantly, it means we only have 12 more weeks together. Do you really want to waste them taking these capricious breaks?" Marcus asked.

Marcus was right. I didn't want to waste the time we had left together, but I also didn't want to play second. "It's been two weeks already, Lace. Is that not a long enough break for now?" Marcus said softly, trying his best to hide his annoyance.

I didn't care that Marcus was bothered. I did care that he had figured me out. "Well, since you are onto me, I guess it is for now, but when I need another break, I'm taking it," I proclaimed.

Marcus agreed not to interrupt my future breaks, and I agreed to let him know when I needed another one. Our friendship and our sexual desire for each other had become undeniable.

I started class two weeks after Marcus. Every day after class, we would meet up to work out and then go back to my room and have dinner. We would stay up talking until we fell asleep in my twin size bed. One evening after an exhausting work-out, Marcus and I walked back to the dorm. "Are you cooking tonight, or do you want to go out?" Marcus asked.

"I'm going to whip something up; I'm too tired to go out," I responded.

"Cool, I'll go shower and be over shortly," Marcus said and departed for his suite.

Entering my suite, I looked in the fridge and realized I didn't have many cooking options. I pulled out a pack of ground beef and cooked up a pot of spaghetti. Marcus had a key to my suite, so I left the spaghetti to simmer while I went and showered. I figured he would probably be done much sooner than I would. As I was showering, I heard pots rattling on the stove. "He must be too hungry to wait for me," I thought.

I continued bathing and began to feel a minor draft. I looked behind me and noticed that the curtain was slightly open. Marcus was standing on the outside of the shower staring at me. He was looking so fresh in his A-line T-shirt and grey jogging pants. Although we had spent plenty of nights together, flirting often and making our way to second base, we had never seen each other completely naked or gone all the way. Against my better judgment, I decided I would change that now.

"Are you going to stare or join me?" I asked.

Marcus didn't respond, but his dick did. It was rock hard. I kneeled in front of him as the water was hitting me from the side and pulled his jogging pants down. My new favorite toy popped out at attention. I slid my tongue from the base of his dick to the top of the head, wrapped my lips around it and began to suck on it slowly, pulling him completely into my mouth.

I used my right hand and moved it up and down in sync with my mouth, while my left hand softly caressed his balls. My tongue played with his head whenever I came back to the top of his dick. I was enjoying the taste of him. I looked up to see whether he was enjoying it, but just as I was looking, he released himself inside my mouth. Marcus' juices were sweet and a little salty, but the mixture tasted so good. A little spilled out as I tried to swallow it all.

Marcus looked at me in disbelief, bent down and kissed me hard. I stood as we were kissing. He pulled away from me slightly and removed his shirt and sweatpants as he entered the shower. I backed up just a little to make room for him. Marcus leaned in close to me, grabbed my ass, and lifted me off my feet.

I felt his cock enter me while he held me suspended in the air. I wrapped my legs around him for support. His manhood felt so good and inviting. He kissed me intimately while he slowly stroked me over and over until I exploded. Marcus let me down, rinsed off, and got out of the shower. "Hurry up, I'm ready to eat," he said, walking out of the bathroom.

My body was limp. I stood in the shower for quite some time. I felt something on the inside but wasn't quite sure what it was. I finished my shower, dried off, and slipped into my robe. I walked to the bedroom to dress and found Marcus lying on my bed naked, pleasuring himself. I smiled, "I thought you were ready to eat?"

"I am," he responded as he got up from the bed and walked toward me. He stopped directly in front of me as I stood in the doorway of my room. He put one hand around my waist and the other over my shoulder. He grabbed me close and pushed the door closed at the same time. He removed my robe and allowed it to fall to the floor.

Then he picked me up and placed me gently on the bed. Marcus spread my legs and began kissing my inner thighs. I could feel his tongue doing circles on my thigh as he moved up toward my pussy. His breath was hot. I felt his tongue enter my pussy. He flicked his tongue over my clit and began to suck hard and fast and then slow and steady. He had a hold of my thighs to ensure I stayed still. Marcus knew his way around my body, even though it was his first visit. I trembled as I climaxed continuously into his mouth. We made love for the first time that day, and it was good. Marcus and I were in Pensacola for two different training programs, and his graduation was approaching fast. Soon, our time together would come to an end.

CHAPTER 3

My brother tugged me out of my thoughts when he pulled off the highway to one of his favorite stops, South of the Border—North/South Carolina state lines. When you're not driving, the ride doesn't seem so bad. Nathan loves to drive. He also loves this rinky-dink South of the Border landmark. It's colorful, old, and run down. I don't know why he loves it so much; more importantly, I wonder how they stay in business. From afar, one would think it is a nice spot, but once you get out and walk around, you realize it is just a big dump.

Over the years, they had added some new stuff here and there. It now looked more like a miniature broke down carnival, instead of a colorful dump. There were several new restaurants, *The Sombrero Restaurant*, which obviously got its name from its looks; a hot dog stand, a sub shop, a diner, an ice cream parlor, and Peddlers Steakhouse. It was dinnertime, and I love a good steak, so we decided to eat at Peddlers. It was a seat-yourself type of establishment. I was cool with that. I picked a booth midway down the restaurant. When I was seated, I could see everything around me, without using too much movement to make it happen.

A young Caucasian woman appeared shortly after we had settled in, setting three glasses of water on the table in front of us. She didn't look much older than 17. Nathan and I were both famished, so we ordered quickly. I ordered a prime rib with a side of macaroni and cheese and string beans. Nathan ordered the exact same thing, which caused me to issue one of my man-killing glares at him. Nathan knew I liked it for everyone at the table to order different food, so I could try multiple items off the menu. He ignored my glare and continued with his order, adding a side of fries and a coke. "And for the boy?" the young waitress asked.

"We're going to share my plate, and he'll have an apple juice."

"No, Mommy!" T yelled.

I continued, "And, I'll take a chardonnay."

"I want a hotdog," T insisted.

"They don't have hotdogs, T. You can eat steak and macaroni with me," I proceeded.

"Mommy, please, all I want is a hot dog," T insisted.

"Two steak dinners and one hot dog coming right up," the young waitress interrupted.

Nathan and I gave each other bemused looks and then laughed as the waitress walked away. We were tickled, wondering how she was going to pull off a steak as a hotdog. I mean, I did it all the time with chicken and pork chops but couldn't wait to see this magic.

T was sitting there, staring intently at his glass of water. He hated water. He thought it was only something you got when you were bad. "Lace, look behind you," Nathan said. I looked over my shoulder and saw our waitress, standing directly in front of the hot dog stand. She reached down into her apron, pulled out some bills, and handed them to the hot dog vendor. I turned back around and saw a huge smile on Nathan's face, "Now that's customer service," he said with a chuckle.

The waitress brought our food to the table on big Texas-sized plates, including T's hotdog, which looked so tiny in comparison. I was so impressed by her service, going the extra mile to ensure my child received what he ordered. I made a mental note to over tip and call the next day and speak to a manager about how great her service was.

Nathan said the grace, and we began to eat. We sat for a while talking, laughing, and joking. We just enjoyed each other's company, catching up on all the time we'd missed being apart.

The sun was starting to set. We took a stroll around the place to walk off some of the food before heading back to the truck. We only had eight hours left to go, and Nathan was determined to finish the ride that night. It's a good thing he didn't need any company because we weren't 10 minutes into our ride before T was asleep. I stayed up just long enough to see the Georgia state line before I dosed off.

#####

Pensacola 2001

We had just finished a base fun run; my legs were weak, and I was drenched with sweat. I don't know why the hell they call it a fun run. It's never fun for me! I walked in my room, popped open a Corona, and plopped onto my chair. "Hey, do you have another beer?" Marcus asked, walking in directly behind me.

"There's Corona in the fridge," I responded. Marcus opened a beer, and we drank and talked as we normally did. We discussed the plans for the weekend as Marcus' son and girlfriend would be flying up to attend his graduation.

"I know it will be a difficult weekend for you, Lace, and I'll try hard to shelter you from as much as I can," Marcus proclaimed.

Alysa, Marcus' girlfriend, decided to come to the graduation at the last minute, and now all the hotels were booked. It was quiet for a few minutes as my thoughts went wild. The three of them would be my neighbors for the weekend.

I was so scared and nervous about Marcus leaving and more nervous about seeing him with her. He graduated the next day, and he had received his orders to Norfolk, VA. I could only hope to get orders back to VA once I completed my training. I was in mid-thought when I felt Marcus' tongue in my mouth. It kindled something inside of me. His tongue played with mine for quite some time. I felt the tension leaving my body as his hand drifted to the waist of my compression shorts, sliding them off. He entered me with two fingers circling and playing with my clit. He stopped for a second to remove my shirt and my sports bra as I sat and watched him, making no attempt to undress myself or him.

He grabbed both my legs pulling me to the edge of my seat and closer to him. My pussy was exposed. His fingers found their way back to my clit, followed by his face. His fingers slid down to my ass as he French-kissed my pussy intently. Almost as if he would never taste her again. He then began to suck on my clit while fingering my asshole. I was so excited, and my mind was clear. The tension and all my concerns escaped through my shaking legs and my pussy as I climaxed in his mouth.

Just when I thought we were done, he stood up and removed his clothes and motioned for me to get on the bed. I lay on my back and spread my legs, and in one scoop, he flipped me over onto my stomach. Marcus spread my ass cheeks and began tongue fucking me in my ass.

I was losing my mind. I had never experienced this type of sex before. My asshole was nice and moist; he took that opportunity to slide his hard dick right in. He was slow and steady, as it was my first time. It didn't take too many strokes for Marcus to cum.

We climaxed together as if it was our last time, sweaty and stinking from our run. It was perfect and much different from any other time. It was emotional and draining. We never showered. We lay in bed, holding each other the rest of the afternoon, in silence. Neither one of us said it, but we knew it was good-bye.

It was now Friday morning. I woke up to Marcus, kissing me on my forehead. "Hey, sweetie! I love you. I'm going to go shower then head to the airport. I'll see you when I get back," Marcus said, walking out of my room. I wanted to scream, "DON'T GO, LEAVE HER THERE!" but instead, I just smiled. The moment of truth had arrived. I jumped out of bed, showered, and got ready for class. Every Friday was a half-day. I wished today wasn't one of those days. I was in no rush to meet Alysa.

Class went by way too fast. I wasn't ready to go back to face my weekend neighbors, so I hung out with some of my classmates. After a few hours with them, I was ready to head back to my room. "The weekend is going to be hell, but I think I have mentally prepared myself to be as phony and as friendly as I can be." I made it into my room without being seen.

I tried to make as little noise as possible, so Marcus wouldn't know I was home. The walls were paper thin. I undressed down to my panties and T-shirt and sat in my recliner. I just needed a minute to clear my mind, while I prepared my heart and soul for the inevitable. As soon as I got comfortable, I heard a loud sturdy knock on my door. *Dammit!* I knew it was Marcus and his foe ass family. I slipped on some shorts and went to open the door.

Alysa stood there next to Marcus holding their son, Marcus Jr's hand. To my surprise, she was very unremarkably looking. Alysa was short, about 5'2. She had a short haircut, and her skin was a pecan brown. She had small lips that were home to a somewhat crooked smile. Her eyes were big, a pretty, light brown. She had a small waist with big hips and a big ass.
Marcus smiled and hugged me. "Lace, I'd like you to meet my girlfriend, Alysa, and son, MJ."
Alysa surprisingly came right in for a hug and said, "It's so nice to finally meet you, Lace. I have heard so much about you. Marcus told me you have been taking really good care of him, just like a big sis."
"It is nice meeting you too, Alysa. I have heard so much about you as well," I responded through a forced smile.

That was a lie. I hadn't really heard anything about her. Once I found out she existed, we agreed not to discuss her. It was just easier that way. "Why didn't you come to the graduation ceremony?" Marcus asked.
Marcus could always tell when I was lying when I looked directly at him, so I faced MJ and played with him while I responded. "My classmates wanted to hang out, so I just went with them for a bit. I thought you guys would have been hanging out too."
"Well, actually, I was hoping we could all go out to dinner," Alysa said. Marcus was standing slightly behind Alysa. He shrugged his shoulders and threw his arms up in a manner as if he couldn't help what was happening.
"I would love to, Alysa, but I think you guys need some time alone. I mean, you have been apart for so long. I don't want to come between y'all."
"Well, OK," Alysa said, "but promise you'll go to the beach with us tomorrow. I've never been, and I'm really looking forward to going." "Pinky promise," I replied, holding my pinky out. And with that reassurance, they were gone.
I sat back in my recliner, and a feeling of uneasiness came over

me, then I heard my door open. It was Marcus. He used his spear key to enter this time. He walked in and sat on the bed without saying a word. "What did you do with the family so quickly?" I asked.

"Alysa is putting MJ down for a nap. He missed his nap time earlier," he replied.

"Did you need something?" I asked.

"Not really, just wanted you to know that I love you, Lace. I know this situation isn't ideal, but I truly love you," Marcus replied as he sat on the edge of the bed.

Marcus then leaned in and kissed me slowly. We kissed for what felt like an eternity. His hand found its way inside my shorts to his favorite spot on my body. He stood me up and slipped my shorts off. He then stood up directly in front of me and pulled his pants off and sat down promptly. I sat on top of him, straddling him, with one leg on each side. I rode him slowly as he took my right breast into his mouth. I could hear Alysa and MJ playing next door.

Marcus held me tightly, moving his mouth from breast to breast as I rode him until we climaxed. I stayed on top of him, hugging him tighter than ever before, while his penis softened inside of me. I eventually released him, stood up, and climbed back onto my recliner. "I love you too, Marcus. I think you should head back next door. I'm sure she's looking for you by now," I whispered. Marcus put on his pants, kissed me on my forehead, and walked out the door. One would think I would feel guilty, but I did not. I was in love with Marcus. I had fallen head over heels in love with him.

I didn't see Marcus for the rest of the evening. I was hot and frustrated. Marcus and his foe ass family were up most of the night, which meant I got no sleep either. I heard daddy more times than I ever wanted to in life. I rolled over and looked at the clock. It was 6:34 a.m. I decided to sneak out and go for a run. I placed my feet on the ground to force myself out of bed. I pulled off my nightgown and placed it on the edge of my bed. I stared at my naked body in the mirror and admired how much it had changed over the past few months. I was working out like crazy, and the results were showing.

As I headed for the bathroom to get myself together, I heard my room door open. I immediately thought it must be Marcus. I turned into the bathroom and closed the door. I took my time in the bathroom; I really wasn't ready to deal with Marcus this morning. I needed some Lace-time. I was really hoping Marcus would talk Alysa out of wanting me to go to the beach with them. I didn't know why she wanted to hang with me. After brushing my teeth, washing and drying my face completely, I slowly opened the door and exited the bathroom.

Walking toward my room, I was startled when I saw Alysa standing there. I was stark naked. She didn't knock, so how did she get in? "Good morning," I said, acknowledging her presence.

"Good morning. I wanted to work out this morning, and Marcus told me to see if you were working out. He then rolled over and handed me your room key to see if you were up. Why does Marcus have a key to your room, Lace?" I walked into the room and reached into my drawer for a pair of compression pants. As I dressed, I asked, "Have you looked in his fridge? He never has food or beer. He has a key, so he can have regular access to free food and free booze." Alysa laughed, I chuckled too. I was glad she bought it.

"Does Marcus have unlimited access to seeing you naked as well?" Alysa asked with a straight face.

"No, he doesn't! Normally when he comes in, he calls out, so I know he's in here. We have boundaries," I acknowledged.

"Do you really have boundaries, Lace? You guys seem mighty close for two people that just met a few months ago," Alysa questioned.

"I think we do, but if you are questioning it, maybe you should be having this conversation with Marcus," I concluded. I put on a sports bra and a T-shirt and announced that I was going for a run.

Alysa stood as I was leaving and then followed closely behind me. I went to the stairway instead of taking the elevator. I wanted to sneak out the back door. Everyone knew Marcus and I were an item. I didn't want the front desk crew seeing me with his girlfriend. That would just be bad. I tried to keep things light between Alysa and me and drummed up a random conversation. "Do you work out often at home?" I asked.

"I try to, but I really don't get the chance. I'm not normally up this early on Saturdays," Alysa replied.

"Really, even with MJ?" I asked.

"No, he usually sleeps until 10 or so. Marcus told me you have a son also?"

"I do. He's with my mother while I'm in training. I miss him like crazy," I responded while stretching.

"I can only imagine," Alysa replied.

As soon as I finished stretching, I started off with our run. I ran a little slower than normal, so Alysa could keep up. She was doing well, so I picked up the pace. "Let me know if I'm moving too fast for you!" I yelled.

Alysa chuckled, "I can keep up, so run to your pleasure!" And with that, I took off. I needed to run this stress off. I headed toward the back of the base. It was a huge track in the back that led you on a beautiful sightseeing trail.

Alysa kept up well. After five times around the track, we started heading back toward the dorm. We stopped running when we got in front of the dorm. I began to stretch again when I heard Alysa speaking, "I'm surprised I had the energy to keep up. Marcus and I were up all night, making up for the lost time. I missed him so much. And the things he does to my body. My body missed him. All of him!" she chuckled.

We were silent as we entered the dorm. I walked in the front because, for some reason, I no longer cared what the front desk would think. My heart was in my stomach. I was not sure why her comment bothered me so. I must have known they would have sex at some point during the weekend. We stepped on the elevator, and I pushed the fourth-floor button.
"Is something bothering you?" Alysa asked.
"No, I'm just tired. I didn't sleep well last night," I replied.
"I hope we did not keep you up. I know how thin these walls are."
"No, Alysa, you didn't. Well, not really. I heard MJ and Marcus playing most of the night, but it wasn't too bad."

After that comment left my month, I realized that I hadn't heard a sound even remotely close to sexual pleasure from Marcus' room all night. "Was she lying to me to see if she would get a reaction out of me?" The sound of the elevator door opening brought me out of my thoughts. "I think we're going to get ready for our beach day and stop for breakfast on the way. How long before you are ready, Lace?" Alysa asked.
"I think I'll just meet you guys there. I need to run a few errands first," I replied. I got to my room and proceeded to enter when I realized I hadn't brought my key out.
Alysa smiled and said, "Good thing! I have your spare key."
"Yes, it is a good thing," I said through a forced smile.

Alysa let me in and headed next door. I reached in the fridge for a beer and decided I needed something stronger. There was a bottle of tequila in the freezer. I pulled it out and poured myself a stiff shot. I poured the rest of the tequila into a water bottle. I couldn't deal with Marcus and his fake ass family sober. I placed the water bottle filled with tequila in the freezer. "It should be nice and cold by the time I'd be ready to meet up with them at the beach." I peeled off my pants and sat on my recliner. I was overwhelmed. My heart was hurting, and I could feel it palpitating in my chest. I put my head in between my legs and just sat there with my eyes closed.

When I finally opened my eyes, I saw feet, and they weren't my feet. I must have zoned out because I never heard my door open. I looked up into the face of Marcus, and I cried. I cried uproariously. I couldn't stop myself, and I couldn't control it. "What happens when you leave? What are you going to do about us? Are you going to stay with her? Do you love her?" I asked question after question; they flowed from my lips through my sobs. Marcus knelt between my legs and laid his head on my thighs. He never responded to any of my questions. He stayed there silently, while I cried, never acknowledging my pain.

As my tears slowly began to fade, Marcus stood up. "Get up! Clean yourself up and be ready to go in twenty minutes," he said.

"I'm not riding with you. I'll meet you guys there," I said.

Marcus tilted his head sideways, looked at me, smiled, and said, "You will do no such thing. You are emotionally unraveling. I know you won't show up, and I need you close. Be ready in twenty."

At that moment, I decided I wasn't going to subject myself to the foolishness of hanging with my boyfriend's foe ass family at the beach.

"Marcus, I'm not going to the beach. I can't tolerate the sight of you two together. The thought of spending the day with you and her, holding hands and doing whatever fake ass families do sickens me, and I just can't take anymore today!" I announced sternly.

Marcus did not like that. He was upset, and I knew it. "Okay, Lace! I'll tell Alysa that I just want to spend time with her and MJ and really prefer if you didn't tag along. Would that work?" Marcus asked.

"Yes," I replied. Marcus kissed my forehead and walked out the door. A few minutes later, I heard MJ running down the hall.

I was relieved, but a part of me wanted to be there to ensure nothing happened between them. I felt instantly sick at the thought of them being together, and I cried. I cried for hours. I cried so much. I cried myself to sleep. I woke up late afternoon, and I waited for Marcus to come back all night. I never left my room, just waiting, and at some point, I drifted back off to sleep. Hours must have passed. I jumped up out of my sleep frantically. I was scared. I didn't know why, but something just didn't feel right. I looked at the clock; it was 5:14 a.m. I was nervous, too nervous to sit there. I stood up and started pacing back and forth. Marcus did not stop by when he returned yesterday.

I picked up the phone and slowly dialed 4011, Marcus' room. No one answered. I dialed Marcus' cell phone and was sent to voicemail. I began to panic. I called Marcus over 117 times that day, with each call being sent to voice mail.

The rest of my time in Pensacola was sad and lonely. My only hope left was to get orders to Norfolk and somehow find Marcus again.

To add insult to injury, that didn't happen. I landed orders to Maryland instead.

CHAPTER 4

"Mommy, Mommy, we're here. Wake up, Mommy!" T yelled. I woke up in my mother's driveway. I must have fallen asleep.

"You have been sleeping for almost six hours," Nathan said.

"Really? It doesn't feel like I've been asleep that long," I replied. I jumped out of the truck and grabbed T. He was overly excited. My time in Miami would be short, as usual. T would stay with my mom and his dad while I would be in Pensacola for the next three months.

I felt guilty every time I left T, but I knew my sacrifices would provide a better future for him later. My mother greeted us at the door. "Your rooms are ready," she said as she hugged us both. She pointed me in the direction of my sister, Yanni's old room, which was once the room we shared as young girls. Nathan had his old room, which Mom had turned into an office. "Get some rest. We have a full day ahead of us," Mom said as we parted ways.

Nathan and I looked at each other and continued to our separate rooms. "Nathan, thanks for getting us to Miami safely," I said.

Nathan smiled and responded, "It's my pleasure, Lace!" T was right behind me, and then he disappeared. I wasn't worried. I was sure my mom or someone in the house had hold of him.

I woke up the next morning to T shaking me to tell me breakfast was ready. I was still wearing the same clothes I arrived in late last night or early morning. Not sure what time we pulled in. I needed to shower and get my life right. I had a long day ahead of me and needed to be functional. I scrambled through my bags to gather my shower bag and something cute to put on. Not sure what Mom had planned for us, but knowing my mother, I knew it involved a lot of family and friends.

The bathroom was attached to the bedroom that I slept in, so I sent T out of the bedroom to go get breakfast while I stripped and jumped in the shower. In the bathroom, I suddenly became overwhelmed, and tears began to fall. I spent some time just looking at myself in the mirror. I had grown over the past 2 years, physically and emotionally, but for the past two days, my mind had been all over the place.

I had spent most of the ride to Miami, pushing memories of Sargent Hendricks and Axel out of my thoughts and the rest of the time thinking about Marcus. I didn't even know why. I hadn't heard from Marcus since that day I didn't go to the beach with him and his foe ass family. I didn't even know if he was dead or alive. A week or so after he left Pensacola, I heard from the young lady at the front desk that Marcus and his family had packed up in the middle of the night to get a head start on the ride, hoping they would beat the traffic. He didn't even say bye, not even a note. I never saw or heard from Marcus again. I felt a tremendous amount of pain during the rest of my time in Pensacola, and now, I was heading back to the same place my heart was broken.

I finished my shower, got dressed, and mentally prepared to entertain whomever my mother had invited over. I heard the doorbell ring several times while I was in the shower, so I knew it was not just family out there. The house was full of family and friends and more coming in each time I looked up. Nathan and I had a ten-hour drive in the morning, so I was not really looking forward to entertaining all day. At some point, I just wanted to rest. However, I was in the mood for a good meal and plenty of food there was.

The kitchen was laid with every southern dish you could imagine: grits, beer-battered catfish, pork seasoned collard greens, buttermilk fried chicken, okra, mac and cheese, and the list went on and on. "We're having an all-day party. Since you guys wouldn't be here long enough to see everyone, I invited everyone over," my mother yelled when I entered the room. T was in the corner with his other cousins eating mac and cheese. I heard music coming from outside. I walked out back to see who was playing music this time of the morning, well actually, it was afternoon. I must have been extremely tired from the ride to sleep that long. I saw several cousins and high school friends. I laughed and thought it was indeed a party! My cousin, Patty, ran up to me with two shot glasses filled with tequila, "bottoms up, bitch!!!" First shot down. I needed to pace myself if this was going to be an all-day party. I did not want to be drunk within the first five minutes.

Before I knew it, I was seven shots in. I began to feel sick; I needed to get food on my belly. I fixed me a plate of just about everything, sat in the back yard and ate, and talked to friends and family all day until night began to fall. Once night fell, the older folks went inside, and we, youngsters, stayed out playing spades, listening to music, and dancing into the wee hours of the night. At some point during the evening, it all became a blur.

I woke up to my mother laughing loudly and a bunch of jibber-jabber. I would never understand the need for my mother to wake up at the ass crack of dawn and prepare breakfast, but I needed it this morning. My brother and I still had the ride to Pensacola ahead of us, and I hadn't even begun to get T situated. There really wasn't much to do with him since he would only be there over the summer. Although his time would be split between his father and my mother, I felt obligated to do the most. T had everything he could have ever asked for, plus more. He was rotten to the core, but he was my rotten baby, and I'd do anything for him.

Terrance, T's dad, came over right in time for breakfast. Things didn't work between us, partially because he was a random. I met Terrance when I stopped by the gas station on 37 Ave. and 167 Street after leaving the recruiting station in 1998. I believe it was Exon at the time. He wasn't interested in me and thought I was out of his league, and I was, but at the time, I had an open mind. He called me over to the car, where he sat with his friend, and asked for my number, and I gave it to him.

I fucked him for a few months before I shipped off to the Navy. He wasn't even a good fuck, just some basic shit. I kept him on the books for when I would come home on leave or vacation. My first time coming home, right out of boot camp, I got pregnant. I got pregnant from a basic ass random. I was fucking up back then. I'm smarter now.

Over breakfast we talked about my upcoming training and my destination after training. I was heading back to Virginia and was ecstatic about it. VA was my home away from home. After breakfast Terrance separated out T's things. He made a pile for him and a pile for my mother. As Terrance packed up his car, T grabbed my face and kissed me, then told me, "Be good, Mommy, and have fun on your trip. I'm going to see Nana."

And with that, I was childless for the summer. Nathan and I said our goodbyes to the family and friends that came to see us off and re-loaded what we took out of the car the previous day. My mother hugged us as tightly as she always did when one of us departed. She hated that we lived so far from Miami. Thankfully, Simba lived close by, and his kids came by every day to keep her company.

I was sure that Nathan was going to make me drive since he had driven the entire way from Maryland, but instead, he hopped in the driver's seat and buckled up! I was so thankful because, honestly, I thought I was still drunk from the night before. It wasn't long before I started drifting off.

Every now and again, I would hear my brother call my name to keep him company. I guess at some point, he finally let me sleep. When I woke up, we were crossing the Pensacola Bay Bridge. "We're almost there?" I asked sheepishly.

"Yep, right on schedule," my brother replied.

We arrived at Corry, and I checked in at the main check-in, and it was déjà vu all over again, minus Marcus. I planned on making my time at Corry quick and easy this time around with no love interest to fuel me.

After checking in, I was informed that there were no rooms on base and was given the option to stay in one of the local hotels. I chose the hotel right across from the base, Ashton Inn. The hotel was just about out of rooms as well, so they put me up in a one-bedroom suite.

Nathan helped me get settled in. I was thankful for the pull-out sofa in the suite. It gave him a place to sleep for the night before he flew out to St. Louis. I noticed a lot of other sailors at the hotel, all in different training programs. I planned to make the best of the three months I would be in Pensacola. For the most part, I did just that. I entertained a few randoms here and there but didn't allow any of them to get too close. I didn't want to take the chance of finding and losing love all over again at Corry Station. Although, honestly, I was secretly hoping to run into Marcus. I'm sure I didn't still love him, but I needed to see him and be sure I was totally over him.

Three weeks before graduation, I was notified that my new command, National Security Group Activity – NSGA – had assigned me to the John F Kennedy. The Kennedy was doing workups, meaning they were in and out of the sea, preparing for deployment. This was news to me, as I hadn't prepared to leave T for more than three months. My family support system was so strong that I didn't have to worry about it too much, but as a mother, I guess it had become natural for me to worry. I was not in the mood to go straight out to sea, but I was overly excited to get back to Norfolk. Maryland was cool and all, but it was NOT my home!

I thought I would have time to settle in before actually deploying. I missed most of the workups by taking a few weeks of personal and a few weeks of house hunting leave. I took that time to go back to Miami and get T registered for school and settled in, while I would be gone on deployment.

Simba and his wife were expecting a new baby, and the family was thrilled. I left my truck with him since I wouldn't be using it, and his family was expanding. When I finally made it to Norfolk, there was only enough time to find and close on my house. This was my second house. My goal was to purchase a house in every state I transferred to while I was active duty. I wasn't even there long enough to receive my household goods before I deployed. Luckily, Nika, Sasha, and Jen were there and had agreed to take care of everything for me. I trusted these girls with my life, considering all things, and I knew they would make sure everything fell into place.

CHAPTER 5
JEN

It was the week of Thanksgiving, I checked into my first duty station, Carrier Airwing Three – CVW 3. The holiday season was in full swing. I didn't have a family, so I had no intention of going anywhere for the holidays. Well, I did have a family. I just didn't have a relationship with them. My mom gave me up at birth. She didn't give me up to strangers, though. She gave me up to my black side of the family. My mom was white. My father was black. His mother raised me. My grandmother convinced my mother that it was best that a black child was raised with its black family.

My mother was young and scared. She did what she thought was best for me. How else would my hair get done? My blonde, long, thin, stringy hair. That's right; I had a white girl's hair. I had a white girl everything. I didn't have one black feature that distinguished me from being white. It was horrible growing up in my grandmother's house being white. Imagine, being black, or so you've been told all your life growing up in a house full of blacks, coming home from school with a letter about lice. My grandmother tried to beat the skin off me because I brought home a disease that apparently was crawling around in my head. I was so young, I understood me as much as my grandmother did. I too thought it was my fault that little bugs found their way into my hair.

My grandmother used to cake my hair with blue magic to prevent the bugs from coming, but it never worked. The bugs liked the blue magic if you asked me. But neither of us knew enough about my hair type to figure it out. My biological mother, who probably could have provided some insight, had happily moved on with her life, leaving me in her past. She married and had two more kids. In high school, my sister, my mother's daughter, and I became best friends. We did everything together. I would even spend the night over their house. Not as my mother's daughter, though, but as her daughter's friend. I always knew who my mother was; that was no secret. I also always knew that my mother didn't want me. She wanted her other two daughters. I could only assume because they were white and from her husband.

We all lived in the same neighborhood. My sisters and I went to the same school and had the same friends. That was how we became best friends. I didn't try to force a relationship with my mother or her kids. I allowed her to live her happiness. My relationship with my sisters developed naturally and took many turns throughout my life. My father stopped by my grandmother's occasionally, not to visit me, but to visit his family. I was nobody to him. Many years passed before I realized which one of my grandmother's sons was my father. They all just lived their lives, dropping by to visit casually. None of them paid me much mind. It was quite easy to leave them all behind when I joined the Navy. I left Minneapolis and never looked back. I didn't even use my own one phone call, which they gave everyone on arrival at boot camp. I had no one to call who cared enough about me to be concerned about my whereabouts or wellbeing.

A few weeks after checking into my squadron, I was informed that I would be deploying with the USS Truman on the upcoming deployment scheduled for November 2000. My sponsor, Airman Miles, was supposed to deploy, but she had gotten herself knocked up and had been accepted into an entry-level training program. She would transfer to Pensacola shortly after having her baby. Naturally, being the next airman to show up, I was slotted in her place. Airman Miles, Lace was what I called her now, showed me the ropes and introduced me to everyone that I needed to know. She took me under her wing to teach me all she could, as fast as she could, before she delivered. By the time I arrived, she was due any day, but she wanted me to learn everything, and she didn't want anyone else to teach me. We became good friends during that time. I spent the holidays with her and her friends, Sasha and Nika, that year.

I had previously met both during my onboarding but didn't bond with them until after Lace re-introduced us. We all developed our own relationships and became great friends. We hung out often. We would talk all day at work and spent countless off duty hours together. The three of them helped me prepare for my deployment. Not that any of them had deployed or knew what it entailed, but they did the best they could.

I was the first one of the four of us to go on an actual deployment. I wasn't looking forward to it. I didn't know what to expect. I was nervous, I think. I worked with an awesome team, and many of them had completed several deployments. My shipmates—coworkers are what they're called in the civilian world—were cool and helped me get over some of my fears of deploying. A few of us were close in age, so we would usually hang out occasionally. One night, one of the older guys decided to hang out with us. He wasn't old, but older then I was. I think he was 21. However old he was, he was old enough to buy liquor. His name was Robbie. He too was slated for my upcoming deployment. Although Robbie was a few years older than me, I felt like we were equally mature. We liked to do a lot of the same things.

Naturally, we built a friendship that gradually turned into a romantic relationship. I was thrilled about Robbie and me traveling the world together, for free. We saw each other through rose-colored glasses. Robbie was older but not very experienced in sex. I had my fair share of partners in high school and had experienced a lot more than Robbie. He would often try different sexual things that he had only seen in pornos. I remember the first time he went down on me, it was like watching paint dry, but I loved Robbie and was willing to teach him all he needed to know to please me. And I did just that. I taught him everything he needed to know specific to my body and my body only.

The first month of deployment was fascinating. We were in a relationship, but sex on the ship was forbidden. That didn't stop us though, but we had to be careful. We would sneak off the flight deck into one of the fan rooms and have a quick fuck session. I would sometimes sneak him into my berthing when most of the girls were asleep. We would climb into my bottom rack and fuck. It was always just a fuck on the ship. It had to be quick. He was never able to sleep with me; neither was I with him. That made me desire him even more. I was hyped for our first port visit in Italy.

We both took leave for that port visit, so we wouldn't have to stand duty. Robbie went through the Morale Welfare Recreation office onboard the ship and reserved us a room in the city. I was so excited. Of course, we saw the country first. We went on a few tours and excursions and ate plenty of local food. By nightfall each day, we would return to our hotel room. Robbie and I would take turns pleasing each other in the most exotic ways—trying different things along the way to see what worked and what didn't. Most of it was new to both of us. We enjoyed every minute of it together. I saw my future in Robbie.

I didn't get to see much of the world with Robbie. I got pregnant during that first port visit. When we hit our second port call, I was flown off the ship back to Norfolk Naval Base, VA. I was only gone for three months, but I was missed by my girls. Lace, Sasha, and Nika were there to welcome me back. Lace's school had been pushed back twice, so she hadn't left for Pensacola yet. I was grateful. It felt good to be home, but I felt better knowing she was still there. Everyone was excited about my little bundle of joy, and so was I.

SASHA

I was a personnel man in the Navy stationed at CVW-3. Hand-selected to provide the onboarding briefs for newly arrived sailors. My Chiefs and Senior Chiefs loved me. They loved the way I lit up a room and new sailors flocked to me upon arrival. I was the best Personnelman they had. The job really suited my personality. I met all my good friends during onboarding briefs. I met Nika, Lace, and Jen during their first few weeks of onboarding. It was also in one of those onboarding briefs that I met Carter. It was love at first sight when I met Carter.

He was gorgeous, tall, and light-skinned with wavy black hair. You could see his perfectly fit body through his uniform. You could tell he enjoyed working out. After the briefing, Carter immediately approached me and asked me out. He didn't ask if I was married or if I was in a relationship. He didn't care. He saw what he wanted and went for it, and it turned me on. Carter and I got married three months after our first meeting. We knew we wanted to start a family immediately and didn't want both parents deployed. We decided that I would separate from the Navy. Carter and I now had two boys and were trying for a girl.

Our life was great, I often thought. A baby girl would complete our fairytale. I desperately wanted to give Carter a daughter, and he desperately wanted one too. We loved the two boys we had. They were happy and healthy. In due time, I was sure a little princess would make her way, but if God never blessed us with a little girl, we would be fine. It wouldn't be for lack of trying, that's for sure. Our sex life was hot and freaky. We often filmed ourselves having sex and watched it afterward just to see how well we pleased each other. It turned me on every time and kept me wanting him. It's funny how I still fantasized about him. Carter was everything to me. I was so blessed to have found a love like this. Some days I just sat and watched him, so thankful that he chose me.

I loved Carter, and I loved the way he loved our family. My sister, Sonya, just two years younger than me, was also in the Navy and stationed in Norfolk. Carter didn't even blink twice when I asked him about caring for my nephew, Sonya's son, for an extended period. He welcomed him in. When Sonya returned from her 7-month deployment, the plan was for her to stay with us until she bought a new home; preferably, a townhouse near us so our boys and her son could grow up together, going to the same school. Sonya and I wanted to keep the closeness the boys had developed during her deployment.

When we were growing up, Sonya and I didn't have that closeness.

We were extremely close now, and neither of us was sure how our relationship developed, considering we grew up so divided. Our parents' love for Sonya versus their love for me sometimes caused problems between us. We tried our best to keep our parents out of our relationship. It was easier now that we were both in Norfolk, and they were still in Dothan, AL, where we grew up. We typically worked our issues out amongst ourselves, because they always sided with Sonya.

Sonya also saw it as a problem and hated that our parents showed her such favoritism. I was the oldest, but they didn't hide their feelings about their beloved baby girl. They cherished her. She could do no wrong in their eyes. She was golden. Sonya looked more like my parents. She was the perfect mix between the two of them. I looked and had all the mannerisms of my father's mother, beautiful, tall, with long hair and caramel completion. She was thin but naturally cut. She was feisty and vivacious. She drew men to her like no other. I was exactly like her.

My mother hated my grandmother, and I paid the price for looking and acting just like her. Luckily, my grandmother adored me. Anything I wanted that my parents wouldn't provide, my grandmother did. She took great care of me. I spent all my summers and most weekends with her. Sonya would come occasionally, but for the most part, she was glued to my mother's side.

My father often tried to play both sides. He tried to say that he loved us equally, but he did whatever my mother said. Every weekend that I spent with my grandmother, my father made sure he spent just a few hours with just me. I enjoyed those moments the most. My father didn't want me feeling neglected, and for the most part, I didn't. I felt loved, just not by my mother. I often thought, "I can't wait until I have children, so I can show my mother how to love her offspring. I'm going to cherish them and love them equally and uniquely."

My grandmother died in my junior year in high school. My provider, friend, protector, and safety net was gone. I felt lost. My relationship with my mother was in complete turmoil. My father and Sonya were stuck in the middle.

It's not that I didn't love my mother, but I damn sure didn't like her. I knew she felt the same way about me because she often said it. I couldn't wait to graduate high school and get out of the house. My father paid all the bills, and my mother had all the say so. I hated the dynamics of the household, and I had no desire to stay there. I didn't really have a complete plan. I just knew I was going to the Navy to get away from my mother, my dad, and Sonya.

"Let's go to Cheers before we pick up the kiddies," Lace demanded. I was always down for Cheers. I loved Cheers. We all did. We changed at work in the bathroom with the go-bag we kept in our cars. We headed straight for the bar. Lace was meeting one of her randoms whom she was fucking on a regular up there. I can't quite remember his name. I do remember his name started with an A. I only remember that because Lace was fucking three guys whose names began with A at the same time. I don't know how she kept up with all of them. To make it easier for Lace and us, we called them all A. Dummies answered to it too. It was fucking hilarious.

A was going to be in the neighborhood and wanted Lace to meet him there. Lace explained that I would be with her, and we only had a short time before we had to grab the kids from daycare. A insisted we come for a little while since he really wanted to see Lace, and he was in the neighborhood. Go figure, right? No one believed he just happened to be in the damn neighborhood. When we arrived, Jay, a homeboy of said random, was sitting to the left of A.

Jay was handsome, very handsome. If Lace wasn't fucking A, Jay would have surely been on Lace's target list. Instead, she passed him along to me like he was hers to pass. I was immediately attracted to him. He was tall and dark with southern charm and a mischievous smile. Lace and I had been friends for some time now, but we were nothing alike when it came to men. I enjoyed being in relationships; fucking random men was not my thing. I didn't judge my friend, though. I understood and respected her reasoning.

Me, on the other hand, I liked monogamy. I wanted to know whom I was sleeping with on a constant basis, not make the decision as the night fell. I desired to wake up with the same person every day and spend my life with the one meant for me. I believed in real love. I knew Lace did too, but she was still nursing her broken heart from her high school sweetheart and wouldn't allow love in until she was good and ready.

I came from a broken home. My mom was the other woman for years. My dad took care of her as best he could until my mom got pregnant with me. She had the audacity to want to keep the baby. She was trying to trap my dad, but my dad was not ready to leave his wife. As a matter of fact, my father and his wife welcomed me into their home at birth. My dad and stepmom loved me, unconditionally. It was hard growing up, seeing my mother play second fiddle. She did it for years. She loved my dad, unconditionally.

When my mother refused to get rid of me, my dad stopped taking care of her. His attention was focused on me, and he started treating my mom like shit every chance he had. I think my mom's love for my dad was just the desire to be loved by anyone. I also think my mom and my dad still fucked occasionally.

My mom loved me too, but her love was different. It was dependent on how well or bad her relationship with my dad was going in the moment. I didn't want to be like my mom. And I didn't want a cheating husband like my dad. He still cheated on my stepmother. I think she knew it. I can't be too sure, but he really didn't try to hide it. It would be difficult for her not to know it.

Jay and I hit it off extremely well. There was a deep connection between us. A connection that I profoundly desired to have with a man. Not just any man, an available man open to love only me. Jay also hit it off with my daughter, Dawn. We called her DD for short.

She fell in love with him just as I did. DD's father wasn't in the picture, and Jay became the only father she knew. After an intense courtship, Jay and I moved in together. A few months after Jay moved in, I remember calling Lace, screaming into the phone that Jay had proposed to me. She was completely silent on the phone. At that moment, I thought she was jealous. I was achieving something she hadn't. When I think about it now, I probably should have taken that as a sign not to marry him. The following Monday, May 18, 2000, I married the love of my life. We were on cloud nine.

It was a Tuesday, in July, I think, a few months after we got married. I was leaving the base when I got a flat tire. I called Jay several times, but the phone kept going to voicemail. Lamar, a coworker of mine, saw me on the side of the road and stopped to change my tire. I had a donut. "You really need to get a full-size spare tire, Nika," he explained. He put on the spare but didn't feel it was secure enough. "I'll drive your car and follow you to your house. Just to make sure you arrive safely," Lamar continued.

"Sure, my husband should be able to take care of this by morning," I said, assuring Lamar that I'd be good to go to work the following day. I pulled up to the house and pointed to the spot where Lamar could park. I turned off his ignition and got out of the car. I walked over to Lamar and thanked him for changing the tire and following me home.

"No problem, Nika," Lamar said as he tossed me my keys. I stood out for a moment and waited for Lamar to drive off. He waved as did I and disappeared into the traffic.

Lamar and Jay reminded me of each other. They almost looked alike—just a few distinct differences. Lamar was a little older but still very handsome, nonetheless, and he had major sex appeal for an older guy. I looked back toward our apartment and noticed Jay peeking out the window. "I wonder why he didn't answer my calls," I thought.

I opened the door to our two-level townhouse style apartment and walked up the stairs. Jay was standing at the top of the steps looking intense and angry. "I called you," I said.

"Who the fuck was that?" Jay shouted.

"It was my coworker. I had a flat tire and called you several times, but you never answered. My coworker saw me and offered to help me. He changed my tire and followed me home to make sure I arrived safely," I explained.

As the word safely left my mouth, Jay slapped the shit out of me and yelled, "Don't you ever bring another nigga to my house, bitch!" and then walked away.

My face stung! I was horrified, in shock, and livid. Initially, I couldn't even respond. Jay had never spoken to me like that or hit me before. Jay was much taller and bigger than me. I was 5'2 with my boots on and five feet even without. I wore a solid 125 pounds—10 of those pounds were breast only. Jay was about 6'2 220 lbs.

None of that mattered when I launched at Jay. I started swinging and punching him in his back, yelling, "Don't you ever put your motherfucking hands on me again!"

Jay turned around, not fazed by any of my blows, and threw me into the wall. He then walked over, lifted me by my neck, held me against the wall, choking me. I was gasping for air. My feet were dangling in the air. I tried kicking and screaming. Jay punched me in my side each time I tried to fight.

DD ran out of her bedroom, crying, yelling, "Daddy, please stop! You are hurting her." Jay turned around, looked at DD, and loosened his grip. I fell to the floor and began to weep. The next day, I packed up all mine and DD's shit to leave. Jay came home as I was leaving, and he begged, pleaded, promised never to do it again. He even agreed to go to domestic abuse counseling. I stayed. Jay and I had been married four years now. The abuse continued and even got worse with every beating.

CHAPTER 6
SASHA

Lace's household goods came in right after the holiday season. Since Nika, Jen, and I all still worked full time, and the kids were just returning to school, it was going to take us a few weeks if not months, to get Lace's house situated. Sonya had recently returned from her deployment and would have to fill in for my regular routine of getting the boys from aftercare and cooking dinner.

Sonya was willing to help. She took two weeks of leave to find a new house. She went out during the day with her realtor and picked the boys up after school. Sonya was a great help. With her help at home, Jen and I were able to stay late most days which allowed us to complete Lace's house quicker than we anticipated.

Nika went over there during working hours and took care of a lot of the labor-intensive stuff. Jay was adamant about her being home by a certain time. Nika said she had help from work. Whoever it was, Jen and I were surely grateful. It's overwhelming setting up someone else's house. I was so thankful it was finally finished and so ready to go back to my routine. I missed my boys and my Carter

Most nights, by the time I would get home from Lace's, the boys would have already been in bed, not asleep, of course, but in bed, nonetheless. Carter would be relaxing in his recliner, watching the news or a game, sipping on an adult beverage. Sonya would be up in her room, doing whatever she did. I missed my family. I felt like I hadn't seen or spent any real time with them over the past month. "I'm so glad to be home," I announced to no one after returning from Lace's.

Carter laughed, "I'm glad to have you home, honey. Are you guys finally finished over there at Lace's?" he asked.

"Yes," I responded with a huge sigh. I was exhausted, but I had the desire to feel my husband in me. I missed him. "I'm going to shower, meet me upstairs?"

Carter smiled in the most devilish way and whispered, "Of course, sweetheart." That excited me. I showered and took an extra few minutes to shave. Carter loved a bald pussy.

When I got out of the shower, I opted to air dry. I walked into our lavish master suite and noticed Carter had the camera set up and positioned toward the love seat. The love seat sat near the bay window to the far right of the bedroom. He had dimmed just about all the recess lights, except three. The blinds were up, and the curtains wide open. Carter liked putting on shows for the neighbors, and I was always willing to indulge.

Carter was sitting on the love seat just as he had been downstairs when I walked into the house, except now he was naked. Legs slightly open, sipping on something. An adult beverage, I would assume. There was a book to the side of him that he picked up and pretended to read when he saw me. I snickered at the thought. It was so cute. In this instance, I must be the aggressor.

I walked over to the bedroom door to ensure it was locked. It was, of course. He always thought of everything. I turned and headed toward my husband. When I got right in front of Carter, I kneeled before him and pushed his legs open a little wider. I looked back at the camera to make sure I was in view. I kissed Carter's left leg going up from his kneecap to his manhood.

When I reached his balls, I made sure my lips and tongue grazed his balls as I moved to his right leg. I kissed his right leg down and back up, stopping only when I reached his sack. I cuffed his balls with my right hand and gave them my undivided attention, kissing and sucking each one attentively. After his balls were soaking wet from my saliva, I took Carter into my mouth. I loved the taste of him after a long day. I used my tongue to play with his head until he became fully erect. Then I took him fully into my mouth. I didn't use any hands; I wanted him all in me. I stroked his dick with my mouth, sucking and slurping with a purpose.

Carter grabbed my head and pushed himself further inside of me. I shook my head loose from his grip and jumped up when I felt Carter about to release. I turned away from him and faced the camera, then slid my wet pussy on his hard dick and began to ride slowly. Carter attempted to get me where I needed to be by playing with my clit, but he didn't last too long with me riding him. I giggled, "Still only takes a couple of pumps," I said.

"You're so funny," Carter said as he removed me from on top of him and reached under the sofa to grab our bondage straps. My eyes widened. I didn't think it was a bondage type of night. Carter sat me in the center of the love seat in full view of the camera. I felt his cum sliding down my leg. He kneeled and caressed my left leg as he strapped it to the foot of the chair. He then moved to my right leg, caressing it while positioning it to be strapped in. I stared at him intently, patiently anticipating the climax; I knew I was sure to come as I was spread eagle. Carter then reached back under the sofa and grabbed handcuffs.

Obviously, he thought this out completely. He stood up, looked me right in the eyes, and said very sternly, "Lean forward and put your hands behind your back." I felt like I didn't have a choice. I was reluctant as I would not have any way to push him off me if it became too intense, but I complied.

Carter pulled me to the edge of the loveseat and began to slowly punish me for my smart comment earlier. He ran circles around my clitoris, lightly nibbling on it in between tongue flicks and sucking. It drove me fucking crazy, tongue fucking, finger fucking, sucking, and teasing. I was trembling, and he didn't care. When he finally thought I couldn't take it anymore, he grabbed my thighs and buried his face in my pussy in full force. He loved every inch of my pussy.

"I needed that," I mumbled to myself. I had been feeling disconnected from Carter over the past few weeks. I felt like we were out of sync for some odd reason. I had previously woken up a few different times, and Carter wasn't in bed. We always went to bed together.

That's how I knew something was bothering him. When I asked what was bothering him, he would just say, "You have enough on your plate, Sas, don't worry about me! Everything's fine."

I didn't believe it, but I didn't really have a clue of what it could be. But after tonight, I feel more connected to him than I ever felt. Maybe Carter just needed me the way I needed him. I had been distracted lately, worrying about Sonya, Jen, and Nika and trying to get Lace's house together. Maybe Carter felt neglected. "I don't know what it is, but once I dedicate my time back to my family, maybe whatever it is will solve itself."

Carter loosened all my straps and released me from captivity. He reached out his hand to help me up as my legs were still weak. He could probably see them still trembling. Carter pulled me close and kissed me long and gently. He grabbed my hand and led the way to our California king bed. I hated our bed; it was so big, and I wanted to always touch him in my sleep. Carter climbed onto the bed and motioned for me to get on top. I laughed as I climbed on top. "What's funny?" he asked.

"You," I responded. Carter always thought he could last longer after the first round. "Cause you know the first round is just pre-cum," he would say. We made love again, and after we both climaxed, I climbed off him. I laid my head on his chest, and we fell asleep, contemplating watching the video we just made.

"Have a great day, sweetheart," Carter said as he kissed my lips. I was still in bed.

"You too, baby," I responded. I was hoping for some morning glory to get my day started, but I guess Carter didn't have the same thought in mind. I didn't mention it, although I wanted to. It was unlike Carter not to even try for morning sex. I figured he was tired since we were up so late last night or just in a rush.

I slowly got myself out of bed and put on my workout clothes. I was still an avid runner even after getting out of the military. It was a way to clear my mind when I was stressed, and I simply enjoyed running. We live in an upcoming development in Suffolk.

Our community has its own walking trail. Most people used it for running, but there were some groups that would meet up on Saturday and walk the ten miles. I ran it. I would run 5 miles to the end and 5 miles back to the beginning. They were building up like crazy. The homes were beautiful and massive. Even the townhomes were ridiculously big.

We owned a three-story, 5-bedroom 4-bathroom townhome with a basement and two-car garage. It was 4200 square feet. It was just perfect for our growing family. I furnished our house with lavish Italian grade kid-friendly furniture. Every room was painted a different color to fit the purpose of the room, of course. On the walls hung pieces of art by undiscovered or independent artists such as Madam Adrienne Muse. I loved our home and our life.

After my run, I went inside to prepare for my day. I showered and woke the kids up for school. Sonya had duty last night, so I needed to get all three kids together. I had a weird feeling in my gut that I didn't have time to explore it, as I needed to get the kids off to school, and I needed to get to work.

Once everyone was ready, I loaded the kids up, dropped them off, and jumped on Highway 64, heading east. I couldn't shake this feeling in my stomach. I felt like Carter, and I reconnected last night, but something was off. When I got up to use the bathroom last night, he wasn't in bed and this was becoming a reoccurring thing.

"Hey, Jen, it's me, Sasha."

Jen laughed, "Bitch, I know who this is! What's up? Why do you sound like that?" Jen asked.

"I don't know. I have this weird feeling in my gut that I can't shake. It's been here for a few days, maybe even weeks, but I feel like it's getting more intense," I said.

"You're probably just pregnant. Take a test and call me later. Got to go," Jen said as she dismissed my call. I smiled at the thought, but I had already taken two tests. They were both negative.

I was sitting in bed, attempting to finish my end of the year input for evaluation. Jay walked into the bedroom and gave me a look. I knew what he wanted but tried to ignore him. I didn't speak or say anything because it didn't usually take much to anger him. I was naked, and the light from the laptop was shining on my exposed breasts. Jay lay across the bed and started sucking my right breast, not giving a damn about what I was doing. I wasn't in the mood, but I never denied my husband. It's just easier that way. Most times, I could usually get in the mood. It would just take a little creativity. Jay was so aggressive, and that was a complete turnoff. Pussy dried right up every time.

I closed my computer and put it on the nightstand to my left. To soften the mood, I started caressing and kissing my husband's bald head. For Jay, that was his green light. Not that he needed one, he often just took the pussy when he wanted it anyway.

Jay pulled the covers off me and yanked me like a rag doll to the edge of the bed. He spread my legs forcefully and started licking and sucking my pussy. Jay moved up to my clit and started curling his tongue over it fast. That was his way of getting me off.

It would usually do the trick for me, but tonight was different. I couldn't get my mind off Lamar. I faked a major orgasm, so we could move on. If I didn't reach my peak with Jay, there was usually a heavy price to pay. He would feel insulted, and of course, I would be to blame. I was learning how to live in peace with Jay. He was so out of tune with my body that he didn't even notice when I faked it.

I wanted straight penetration at that point, so we could be done, and I could get back to writing my input. Jay had other things on his mind. While I lay there waiting for the dick, Jay walked around the other side of the bed and shoved his dick in my mouth, hard. He was fucking the shit out of my mouth. He kept thrusting himself in harder and harder. I was on my back with my head hanging off the bed. It was very uncomfortable, but he didn't care. He never did. I wondered if Lamar would be this rough and inconsiderate. I daydreamed about Lamar often.

But we were just work friends. I met Lamar three years ago when he checked into the command. I was his sponsor. Jay was having a difficult time cumming, and I was much too uncomfortable to let him continue in his present thrusts. I pushed Jay off me and told him to stick his dick in, already, but I said it nicely. Ensuring there would be no backlash. He walked around to the other side of the bed and demanded I turn over. I did. I liked it from the back. It was one of my favorite positions. Jay shoved his dick in with no regard.

I was only wet because my thoughts were on Lamar. Yes, we were only friends, but we had become disturbingly close over the last year. We spent a lot of time together, not on purpose, in the beginning, and only during working hours. Our friendship started out normally with small talk and work requests. It gradually moved to another realm, of course, without notice or intent from either party. We started going on walks during the day and would sometimes have lunch together. We could sit and talk for hours. He was so intelligent. It turned me on every time he spoke.

Lamar contemplated everything before he spoke and spoke slowly. I was intrigued by that. I would listen as he spoke or just watch him as he sat and thought quietly. Lamar would often put his two fingers above his lip right under his nose when he would think about something. I often imagined he had just finished fingering me and was smelling the lingering scent of my pussy. Truth is, he'd never touched my pussy, not even my thigh for that matter. He never touched me at all, and yet, my pussy was always wet when I was near him. I touched him as often as I could. Nothing intimately! A rub of the back or graze of his hands. I would sometimes walk a little too close, so our shoulders would meet or sometimes sit uncomfortably close to him.

Sometimes, when his hands were cold, he let me rub them to warm them up. He liked the subtle touches but would never be the initiator of any such questionable behavior. We do hug often. Now that we no longer work together, we go out of our way to see each other, but still only during working hours, because spending time together outside of work would be inappropriate and make the friendship more than what it is.

Each greeting was met with a hug that got tighter and closer and lasted just a little longer than the previous hug. Each time we hugged, I got closer and closer to him, hoping to feel his bulging dick, a sign of excitement, or interest, or something, but nothing was ever there. He was too refined to display any type of desire or reaction. I was almost certain during our last embrace that he wanted to kiss me. He held on longer than usual, lingering, tethering the lines of infidelity that neither of us would ever cross.

Jay finally finished fucking me; I was not even sure if he finished or if he was just tired. He shoved me onto the bed like he always did when he was through with me. "I wonder if Lamar would treat me like a piece of meat," I thought silently. "I doubt it. He is such a gentleman. He opens every door and always considers me first. He never tells me no, and I love that." I thought of Lamar nonstop. All-day, every day. We had a crazy inappropriate bond.

When outsiders saw us, they assumed we were married to each other, that is. We both wore our rings proudly. We should release each other from this friendship, but neither of us wants that. The way he laughed at my jokes, and I at his was unachievable with anyone else. We even had our own club, where we were the only two members, with countless inside jokes that we found hilarious.

Two people for sure wouldn't find any of our inside jokes funny at all, Leni, Lamar's wife, and Jay. Lamar and his wife had 6 kids together. Evidently, he loved being in her. He loved her, no doubt. They had been married 15 years, and he had been faithful.

When we spent time together, we didn't talk about Leni much. Lamar didn't talk much when we were together, in general. I sometimes pried information out of him, and I enjoyed it: watching him think, considering every word before he carefully spoke. I imagined he would take that same careful consideration when he opened his mouth to eat my pussy, unselfish and deliberate, yet intense and meaningful.

He was reserved. I was sure there was a lot he wanted to say, but I knew he never would. I was usually very open when we were together. I talked about everything. He knew my entire life. I shared everything with him, everything except how Jay beat me, and how I fantasized about him. I didn't share that part of my life with anyone. Jen, Lace, and Sasha knew about Jay. They'd begged me to leave him. They didn't know the full extent of it. Shit, I didn't think I knew the full extent of it either. But no one knew about Lamar, not even the girls. Our friendship was our little secret; he was my safe place, my happy place, and I wanted to keep him there.

SASHA

It had been almost a month since we finished Lace's house, and I was back into my family routine. Sonya still hadn't found a home of her own yet but was diligently searching. She went out often into the evening with her realtor looking for the perfect place. I offered to go with her, but she wanted to do it on her own. Carter had also been working late on a major project at work. I was home most nights alone with the kids. But something felt wrong.

There was a disturbing feeling in my gut, and I couldn't shake it. Whenever I saw Sonya and Carter together, it would intensify. One night when they both arrived home, within minutes of each other, like they often did, I watched them attentively. They greeted each other with small talk in the foyer and occasionally cut each other an awkward or sheepish glance.

"Are you guys hungry?" I asked. They both answered yes, so I made them both plates. They sat at the table and ate dinner. I went into the family room and positioned myself on the sofa that faced the dining room. I picked up my phone and pretended to play a game. They both glanced at me once or twice, but I ignored it. They enjoyed each other's company with a few hushed giggles in the mix over dinner.

Sonya finished eating first. She stood up to put her plate in the sink and gently put her hand on Carter's shoulder keeping it there, allowing it to move from one side to the other as she moved toward the sink. I felt nauseous. It couldn't possibly be what I thought it was.

I slept miserably, thinking about what I had witnessed the previous night. I phoned Nika and asked her to meet me at Jen's after work. We always met at Jen's because Robbie was just a roommate at this point. We had no respect for him, and we basically had the run of the house. Whenever we all got together, Robbie knew that it was his queue to leave. I think we appreciated him knowing his role. We could talk about anything without men's ears around.

Jen also lived in the middle of all of us. Her house was right off the highway, and the easiest to get to for each of us. I got to Jen's first. "What's up, Sas?" Jen asked.

"Let's wait on Nika," I responded. Nika arrived shortly after. I was sitting at Jen's dining room table, sipping a glass of wine, when Nika walked in. I wouldn't say a word until both were there. "Something's wrong; remember that feeling I couldn't shake?" I said, talking to Jen and Nika.

"Sasha, I'm telling you, you're just pregnant. It's been three weeks since you took the last test. Just take another test," Jen suggested.

"I'm on my period, Jen. I'm not pregnant."

Jen, now a nurse who apparently knew everything about the human body, continued, "Women have their periods all the time while they're pregnant. I have a test in the bathroom," Jen announced as she stood up from the table and started to walk into the bedroom, which she and Robbie shared.

"I'm not taking another fucking test, Jen," I yelled.

"Sasha, what the fuck? What is it? If you know, tell us already," Nika ordered.

I didn't say a word. Not that I didn't want to. I was trying; I just couldn't get it out.

"Do you think this feeling has something to do with Carter disappearing at night? You said it's becoming routine?" Nika asked.

I wasn't sure how I wanted to respond to Nika's question. I knew it was, but I didn't know how to say it, or I didn't want to say it. I didn't want to believe it. Originally, I didn't consider that could have something to do with it. One night, I got out of bed to look for Carter, and I found him in his car on the phone. I didn't really think anything of it. My eyes began to swell, and my lips quivered.

"What the fuck, Sasha? Say something!" Jen demanded. "Do you think he's cheating?" Jen continued.

"Jen, you think everyone is cheating since that shit with Robbie happened," Nika snapped.

"Maybe, Nika. I thought me, and Carter's relationship was strong. I thought we loved each other immensely. I never thought, in a million years, he would ever cheat on me," I responded through quivering lips and swollen eyes.

"Sasha, slow down. You don't know that he's cheating for sure," Nika commented.

"Give me your laptop, Jen?" I asked through my cracking voice. My eyes were full of tears, falling one by one, dropping silently on the table. Jen walked over to the island reluctantly, grabbed her laptop, and handed it to me.

"I have a bad feeling about this," Jen announced.

"Me too," Nika said.

"Last night, when Sonya and Carter arrived home, minutes apart as they had done over the past few weeks, I watched their interaction over dinner. They were comfortable with each other. A level of comfort only I should have with Carter. They were cozy, sneaking peeks at each other and giving each other elusive glances. It made me so sick I threw up," I said as I was logging into our AT&T account, "I looked at Carter's call detail." Once I was completely logged in, I turned the laptop around so Jen and Nika could see.

There were over 3,000 calls and texts between Carter and Sonya starting the same week she returned. After 7:00 p.m., when the minutes were free, was when they did most of their talking. They talked for hours. Those nights he was getting out of bed coincided with her duty days. Most of the calls took place when one or the other was on duty.

While he worked late, and she was out looking for a house, there were no calls between them. That must be the time they spent together. Nika and Jen were dumbfounded. They couldn't believe it and thought there had to be some type of explanation.

"Sonya would never do that to you. It's impossible," Jen explained.

"Explain it to me then?" I asked, crying rumbustiously. Neither of them had an explanation. Nika stood up and hugged me as I sat there. I heard her speaking almost in horror.

"I saw Sonya and Carter out near the beach. They both spoke, and it looked innocent, I didn't think anything of it. I should have mentioned it when I saw it."

I looked up at Nika, "When, when was this, Nika?" I asked.

"I can't remember exactly, Sasha, but it was more than three weeks ago, and it was during the workday, so I completely dismissed it."

"No, I don't believe it. You need to ask them about it, Sasha. I'm sure they will have an explanation. It doesn't make sense for Sonya to do that. I just can't believe it, Sasha. There must be an explanation," Jen concluded.

Nika was silent, just holding me, allowing me to cry. Jen was pacing back and forth in disbelief until she too broke down and began to cry.

CHAPTER 7
JEN

I couldn't help but cry. I felt Sasha's pain. It was real to me. No, I wasn't married to Robbie, and it wasn't my sister he slept with, but my pain was just as real. Maybe not, though. Sasha loved Carter for real. Like on a different level type of love. I didn't know that type of love. It was the type of love where she literally lived her life for him. Not that it was a bad thing, but it was emotionally draining just watching the amount of effort, time, and energy she put into her marriage. Maybe that's why Robbie cheated. I was not capable of displaying love like Sasha, partially because I had never seen it growing up or understood it.

When Robbie returned from deployment, in the summer of 2001, we moved in together. We got a two-bedroom apartment near the highway off Northampton. Alisha, our daughter, was born a few months before Robbie's return. After Alisha came along, things changed for us. I was focused on being a mother and starting a family. I had also decided to get out of the Navy and pursue a degree in nursing.

Robbie, on the other hand, still wanted to party and hang with his friends every weekend. We were completely different people. We had grown completely apart in the first year of Alisha's life. Regardless, I was dedicated to raising our daughter in a happy home.

I was stationed at Fleet Squadron Six or VC-6 Norfolk, riding out my time with two months left before I separated. My section leader, Petty Officer Jill McKnight, was being just as petty as the title she carried, "Petty Officer." The miserable bitch scheduled me for the overnight watch. We were deployed together on the Truman, and we worked well together. I didn't remember her as the petty type, but she proved me wrong.

Typically, with less than 60 days left on active duty, you would come off the watch bill, but not with this trifling bitch. I didn't know what it was, but it was something about me she just didn't like. Luckily, I was scheduled to be on watch with Hernandez. He was cool as a fan. He typically didn't mind you skating out of duty if you could be reached at a moment's notice. I lived about 10 minutes from the base. It was easy to do. Watch started at 2345. I planned to be heading back to my house by 0130 to sleep in my own bed.

"What time do you want me back?" I asked.

"Be back by 0500," Hernandez replied.

"Sweet," I said as I walked out the door. During the drive home, I felt uneasy and prayed to God I was not pregnant. I had just had an abortion a few months earlier. I didn't tell Robbie. I did not want him to talk me into keeping it. We had Alisha, and I was separating from the military, and in school full time. We couldn't take the chance of bringing another baby into this relationship.

When I arrived home, I observed that there was a car parked in my spot, a familiar car, but I couldn't put my finger on it. I was tired and too exhausted to try and figure it out. "It is probably one of the neighbor's guests," I thought to myself. I opened the sliding door to my patio because we never locked it and used it as the front door. Everyone entered through the patio door. I walked inside, and my apartment was pitch black. I expected Robbie to be up watching TV. "He must be in bed," I thought to myself. I decided to nap on the couch, so I wouldn't wake him.

As I was lying there with my eyes close, I kept hearing irregular sounds coming from the back of the apartment but wasn't sure what it was. I rolled off the sofa and went to check on Alisha. She was sound asleep. As I stood there, it occurred to me that the sounds were coming from my bedroom. The bedroom I shared with Robbie.

I walked less than 20 feet toward my bedroom, and the irregular sound became a little louder and a bit familiar. I put my ear to the door, thinking, "Maybe he's watching porn," as I listened. I thought about that car that was parked in my parking spot, and I pushed open the door. I hit the switch on the side of the wall, so I could see what the fuck was going on. As soon as the light came on, I heard, "What the fuck?" I looked to where the sound had come from and saw my section leader's titties and ass, straddled across Robbie in my bed.

My heart hit the roof, beating a thousand miles a minute. I stood there in surprise for what felt like an eternity. I couldn't believe it. It was a complete out-of-body experience. I literally saw myself fly across the room and knock that bitch straight off his dick. I just remember stumping and kicking her and Robbie, pulling me off her. When she finally got from under me, I saw her picking up what she could find of her things and screaming to the top of her lungs as she ran out of my patio door. Clearly, it wasn't the bitch's first time here.

I ran after her ass, and Robbie ran after me, naked. She jumped in her car, parked in my fucking spot, and drove off. My rage then turned to

Robbie. I ran in the house and grabbed the first weapon I could find, a cast-iron skillet still sitting on the stove from dinner I made earlier. I wonder if this asshole fed his bitch my damn food. There was still food in the pan, but I didn't fucking care. As soon as Robbie ran into the house butt ass naked, I swung it at him, landing it right across his head. He charged me and contained me. That fueled my anger even more. I literally tried to fucking kill Robbie.

"You had this trifling bitch in my parking spot and in my bed?" was all I remember screaming. Robbie got control of me and locked me in the bathroom. A few of the neighbors heard the noise and called the cops.

I became angrier and angrier as I paced the bathroom floor. Then I just collapsed onto the cold floor. I cried. I cried, and I cried. In the midst of my tears, I heard Robbie speaking with someone. I wasn't sure who it was until I silenced my tears. "No, officer! The noise isn't coming from here. I'm not sure where the noise came from, but I did hear the commotion," Robbie explained.

I was supposed to go back on duty that morning. Instead, I called Hernandez and told him what happened. He told me to stay home and deal with what just happened, and he would take care of the rest. I packed up Alicia, who slept through the entire ordeal and went to Sasha's. Sasha stayed up all night with me as I cried.

I was 2 months shy of obtaining an honorable discharge from the Navy. My chances were shot now. I just knew I was going to Captain's Mast for dereliction of duty and beating that married miserable bitch's ass. I arrived on the quarterdeck, looking like a bag of ass. I was mentally prepared for whatever punishment might transpire.

I walked in, expecting to be escorted to the Command Master Chief's office. That was always the first stop before Captain's Mast. I stood there for a moment, waiting for instructions, the quarterdeck officer looked at me puzzled and said, "Airman Adams, do you need something? Why are you standing there looking retarded?" I looked around, still unsure of what was about to happen. After about 30 seconds, I walked through and went to my desk.

I sat there for over an hour trying to figure out what the holdup was, and then Hernandez walked up. "Hey, are you OK?" he asked.

"Yes, I'm fine. I'm just a little perplexed trying to figure out why I haven't been called into Master Chief's office yet," I responded.

"I took care of it. I told you last night that I would," Hernandez said. Puzzled, I asked, "What do you mean you took care of it? What's going to happen, am I going to mast?" I had a lot of questions.

"No, you are not going to Captain's mast; nothing is going to happen. I spoke to McKnight, and we both agreed that we wouldn't report each other. She won't report me for allowing you to leave, and I wouldn't report her for adultery. Some of us really do take care of our Sailors."

I rolled my eyes from a place deep within my soul. "They take care of your boyfriend too," I said.

Just as the words left my mouth, my desk phone rang. It was Sasha. "Jen, we need to head up to Maryland. Mrs. Thompson called and said Lace really needs us."

I was so over the Lace and Marcus bullshit, I snapped, "Damn, Sasha! I have my own shit to deal with. I really don't know if I can deal with Lace and Marcus drama. When the fuck is she going to get over it? He's not coming fucking back. She needs to get over that shit. It's been almost a year."

"No, Jen. Don't do that!" Sasha interrupted. "You do not have the right to determine how long she can hurt. Her pain is hers, and it's real to her. If you don't want to go, fine, I understand, considering…but this you cannot do," Sasha concluded.

Sasha was right, but I didn't give a fuck. I was hurting too. I just caught my man literally fucking another woman in my bed, 20 feet from our daughter's room. My pain was real too. "What makes Lace's pain more real than mine?"

The phone line was silent. Sasha must have sensed my thoughts. "Jen, I'm sorry about Robbie. I truly am. I'm sorry that you're hurting. Maybe a weekend away from it all is what we need." I did not want to be without Sasha and Nika this weekend. I needed them. They were my moral support. They were my family.

"I think it will be good for the three of us to meet up with Lace and just get away," Sasha continued. Sasha dismissed my pain so easily because she didn't think Robbie was good enough for me. She never liked Robbie; actually, none of the girls did. They tolerated him for me and Alisha's sake.

SASHA

Jen and Nika spent the evening trying to calm me. I tried to calm down, but every time the tears stopped, I would think of Carter or Sonya or both, and the tears would swell in my eyes again. I was hurt, and I was livid. I didn't call Carter or Sonya to tell them I wouldn't be home in time to pick the boys up from aftercare. I saw the school calling my phone, but I couldn't muster up the strength or energy to answer. I lived 40 minutes from Jen, and with traffic, it could easily be an hour plus. There was no way

I would make it before six either way. Jen, Nikka, and I sat in silence for over an hour.

Nika finally broke the silence announcing she had to go grab DD, and she offered to grab Alisha from aftercare. Jen accepted and sat with me, holding me. "What am I going to do?" I asked as Nikka was leaving? Neither of them answered. They just looked at me pitifully. I loved Carter and had no idea what my next move would be without him.

Jen finally spoke, "What if it's not what we think, Sasha?" What if what Nika saw was innocent? What if there is an explanation as to why there were so many phone calls?"

I knew what Jen was doing, but it wasn't working. I, too, had looked for the "what ifs" before I decided to tell them about it. There was no valid explanation.

Jen spoke again, trying her best to calm me, "Maybe you should try talking to them both, Sasha, just to be sure."

I ignored Jen; I was over her suggestions. "I need to speak to Lace. She would know what to do," I whispered.

Jen, with her voice raised a little, said, "Sasha? No one, not me, Nika, nor Lace, can tell you what to do. You have to make the decision for yourself. And what are you going to do, wait three months for Lace to return before you do something?"

Jen was right. I needed to talk to Carter and Sonya. I stayed at Jen's until Nika arrived back with Alisha and DD.

Nika and I walked out at the same time. Nika hugged me tightly. "We'll get through this," she said. I drove home in silence, no radio, just my thoughts. "How will I approach them? "I wondered."

When I arrived home, both Sonya and Carter were there in the kitchen cooking dinner laughing and having a good time together. "This motherfucker has never lifted a hand to help me in the kitchen," I thought to myself.

 Carter looked toward me with concern on his face. "Sasha, where have you been?" he asked. "We have been blowing your phone up," he continued.

I grabbed my phone out of my purse to see if Carter was blowing smoke up my ass. He was not. I had 12 missed calls between him and Sonya and one from my mother. I didn't answer Carter's question. Instead, I blurted out, "Why the fuck are there over 3000 calls and texts between you and Sonya? I checked the call log on our phone account, Carter. I saw that you two have been having a lot of late-night conversations. Are y'all fucking?" I asked.

They unequivocally denied it. Sonya was even appalled that I would ask her something like that, and Carter became completely defensive. I became furious. "Why the fuck are there so many calls between you two then?" I asked again.

"You're tripping, Sasha! I can't even believe you would ask me that," Carter said. "We're fucking family," Sonya screamed before she stormed out of the kitchen and up the stairs.

I wanted to follow behind her and yank her ass back down, but I couldn't. I wanted Cater to come up with something grand to make me believe him. He did not. He stopped what he was doing, grabbed his jacket near the door, his keys off the key rack, and walked outside, mumbling, "Unbelievable!"

Sonya called my parents crying and screaming that I was accusing her and Carter of having an affair. As usual, my parents had the audacity to think that I was so jealous of my baby sister that I would make up a story about her sleeping with my husband. I couldn't believe it. The last thing I wanted to do was ruin my family. "*What now?*" I thought. They both denied it, I had no proof, and we were all mad as hell.

Carter and Sonya got a kick out of my parents thinking I was making up an affair and threw it in my face the next couple of days. I was livid. They were playing on my emotions. I was enraged. I was so sick and devastated. I didn't know what to do.

Neither Carter nor Sonya apologized. They walked around my house, being extra friendly to each other, cutting me completely out of all conversation, as if nothing had happened. But I knew it had; I wasn't crazy. I emailed Lace. No telling when she would respond, as the systems were often unpredictable out to sea.

Hey Lacey,

I hope you're doing well. Did you get the care package we sent? The cranberry is your favorite, and the grapefruit is your second favorite. Small talk over. Short version: I think Carter and Sonya are having an affair. They denied it. Like literally dismissed my thought. Now they are both walking around my house like I'm insane, cracking stupid jokes, making smart ass comments. There are over 3000 calls and texts between the two of them. Nika saw them out but didn't tell me until after I told her about the calls. She said it looked innocent enough, and she didn't think anything of it at the time. Carter has been leaving our bed during the middle of the night. One night, I went to look for him and found him in his car on the phone. Jen, I don't think it's possible for Sonya to fuck my husband, but Lace, I know she did. I had a weird feeling in my gut for weeks before I found out. I wish you were here; I know you would know what to do. I'm manic, and I feel like no one has my back. You should have heard my parents' reaction and ridicule of me accusing my sister of something they knew she would never do. Lace, I feel like I'm losing my damn mind and my family.

Love and miss you,
Sasha

I was sitting at work, staring at my phone screen when an email popped in from Lace. I was so excited she responded so quickly.

What the FUCK, Sasha!! Listen, Sas, it's hard for me to believe that Sonya or Carter would do something like this too, but the truth is you never know. Even people with all the love in the world sometimes mess up. If they are denying it, the only thing you can do is catch them in the act, but understand, once you do, there is no going back. The question is, do you really want to know? If they were and you called them out on it, I'm sure it has stopped. It could have been a mistake or minor indiscretion leading up to something inappropriate. If it wasn't a mistake, and they are, then they will continue. Jen watches her nanny through nanny cams. Although she hasn't had a nanny for quite some time, I think the cameras are to watch Robbie, but that's neither here nor there at the moment. She has several of them strategically placed around the house. You don't notice them, and they can be placed anywhere. If you really want to know the truth or just need peace of mind, that's an option. If you decide to go that route, I pray you find nothing.

I love you, girl!
Lace~

I knew Lace would have the answer. I called Jen to see what she had planned after work. Jen had no plans. I headed for her house after I got off, and she showed me all the cameras she had hidden.

"Where did you get them from?" I asked.

"Mostly online," Jen responded. We immediately ordered several for my house. I didn't want Carter or Sonya to know, so I had them delivered to Jen's. A few days later, Jen received the package.

The following day, while Carter and Sonya were still at work, Jen and I headed over to my house. We hid the cameras deliberately throughout the house. I hadn't spoken to my parents in over a week, and conversations with Carter and Sonya were at an all-time low as well. The tension was at an all-time high in the house.

The cameras had been in place for almost two weeks. I was scared as hell to watch them. They would have to be crazy to do anything there. I could easily walk in and catch them, I thought. Then I thought about Robbie. My schedule was predictable. If they really wanted to, I guess they could find the time.

I didn't know what I would find on the cameras, and more importantly, I didn't want to lose my family. I loved my husband very much, and I didn't want to lose him. I also loved my sister and didn't want to lose her. I was hurting, though. The feeling in my gut was more prominent now than it was ever before. I didn't know if I was more hurt by Carter, or Sonya and my parents.

My parents threatened to drive up and move Sonya out of my

house. They did not want her subjected to my idiocy. They wanted me to apologize and let this silly notion go. I laughed at their delusion. I sat quietly, contemplating watching the cameras.

Nika called and interrupted my thoughts. I told her what Jen and I had done and that I was too scared to watch the clips. She suggested we watched them together. "If there is something alarming on the cameras, you should not be alone when you see it," Nikka exclaimed. "If you don't see anything questionable, maybe we can all agree to put this behind us. Apologize to both Carter and Sonya and move forward," Nika concluded.

I partially agreed, and we made plans to meet at Jen's later that evening. The three of us watched the clips while drinking wine that Wednesday evening.

My parents made good on their threat. They arrived Saturday morning. I greeted them at the door with hugs and smiles. I hugged my dad extra tight. My mom and I did our same usual side hug. Sonya was moving out because I had not apologized in the allotted time frame bestowed upon me by my mother. "I hope you guys plan on staying," I mentioned. "I have a full day planned for us as a family."

My mom turned her nose up as she does then gave me a half-ass smile and asked, "Have you come to your senses, Sasha?"

"I sure have, Mom, and I'm going to apologize in front of everyone tonight." Her smile turned genuine. She was pleased.

I made an entire day of the apology I was going to give. I went grocery shopping and brought all the ingredients to make Carter and Sonya's favorite meal. Around 4 p.m., Jen and Nika arrived. We prepared the table for dinner and chatted amongst ourselves. My mom, dad, Carter and Sonya sat in the family room, and all caught up, and laughed at my insinuation. Once the table was prepared, I called everyone into the dining room. Carter led the prayer and blessed our home, growing family, and forgiving hearts. I wasn't pregnant, but it was still his desire. We ate and drank and had a great family dinner.

Shortly after dinner, I sent the kids upstairs to watch TV. I invited the adults into the family room for a movie not suitable for the kids. I pulled a freshly produced DVD out of its sleeve and placed it gently into the DVD player. Had to be careful, didn't want it to get scratched. I found a seat on the arm of the sofa right next to my loving husband. I hit play on the remote I held in my right hand. I had a professional fuse all the clips from the nanny cameras together, and he added some background music at my request for shits and giggles.

I, Jen, and Nika watched my family: my mom, my dad, my sister, and *my husband,* in awe. Their faces were twisted as they watched the fucking show. It was full-blown porn, starring Carter and Sonya. It started with Sonya coming into view right after I left for work one Saturday morning. She crawled into my bed, kissed Carter passionately on the lips, working her way down to his thick shaft while putting her ass on his face. She tried to suck the fucking skin off his fucking dick.

And he pleased her orally just the same. They were both very impressive. A part of me wondered if they had taped this session. He got off, right in her mouth. It was hours' worth of clips of Sonya sucking and fucking my husband like he was hers. He fucked her every which way to Sunday.

She took it up the ass like a fucking pro. "Turn this shit off!" my mother screamed. It startled me for a second. I looked at my mother, smirked, and turned the volume up to its max. Yea, I was hurting, but no one was going to make a fool of me in my damn house.

CHAPTER 8
LACE

"Reveille, reveille. All hands heave out and trice up," the quarterdeck watch announced over the public-address system. "I hate those fucking words," I thought to myself as I flickered my eyes to the bright lights turning on. It was my last day waking up in this 6x2.5 middle rack. I prayed it would be my last deployment. It had been a long 243 days, and I couldn't get off this ship fast enough. We were only supposed to be deployed for six months, but it was extended several times over.

The rocking of the ship as it pulled into the dock excited me. I was so thankful that I finished packing the previous night and slept in my clothes. I jumped out of my rack into my shoes. I reached for my first sea-bag and threw it on my back. I grabbed my other bag and headed for the brow. We must be close to the dock. The sounds of the waves crashing against the sides were drowned out by the sea of people on the pier. Yells, screams, and laughter filled the air.

The smell of the fresh air, as I stepped off the brow, was intoxicating. It felt good to be on American soil. I started my count down the first day of deployment. It was a sad feeling leaving everything behind, not knowing whether or not you would return. My thoughts were abruptly interrupted by a screeching yell, b.i.o.t.c.h!!!! I turned around to see Jen and Sasha running toward me.

I chuckled, "Leave it to these two to find me in a sea of people." We hugged, laughed, and looked one another up and down, making sure everything was intact. After all the bullshit that happened while I was gone, I took an extra-long look at Sasha, and she looked great. It took us 50 minutes to find Jen's car and another hour to get off the damn base. I was so ready to just get to Jen's. We had a night of partying and drinking ahead of us, and I was ready to get it started.

I called my mom and Mrs. Thompson on the way to Jen's to let them know that I had made it back safe and sound. I told my mom about my travel arrangements to pick up T and informed them both that I would be unavailable for the weekend. "I'm going to hang with my girls and just have a great time."

"Listen, Lace," Mrs. Thompson said sternly, "don't be out there entertaining Joe, Bob, and Billy this weekend. Get your ass somewhere and sit down. And Lace, don't kill anyone this weekend, on accident or on purpose!" I laughed. She knew me so well.

"Will do, Mom," I said as I gave her a salute through the phone. I called her mom each time she acted like my mother. They both acted so much alike.

Jen drove from the port of Norfolk to her house. I opted to go to Jen's for the night instead of having someone drive me to my house in Chesapeake. The traffic was going to be crazy, and I wanted no part of it. I hadn't even seen my house since my furniture was delivered. Sasha, Jen, and Nika unpacked and set everything up. They knew me well enough. I'm sure they did a wonderful job.

It took us almost two hours for a 20-minute ride to maneuver through traffic. We made a quick stop by an ABC store before reaching our destination. We pulled up to Jen's house and was quickly met by Nika with shots of vodka and tequila, my kind of welcoming home party. We tossed up the idea of staying in and catching up or going out. Apparently, there was a lot I needed to be filled in on. But I wanted to get fucked, and neither of them could do it for me. Collectively, we decided to go out and find me some prey. We laughed at the thought and continued taking shots.

After taking way too many shots, everyone was finally dressed and ready to go. We must have all believed it was still summer out because we were certainly dressed like it. Sasha was always a show stopper and always almost naked. Even after having two kids, her body was still amazing. She wore an aqua front draped and backless top that showed off her glowing caramel skin and small waist. Her big ass and hips protruded through her cut off booty shorts. Her hair fell right to the center of her back. It was thin but very long and wavy. Sasha finished her outfit with a pair of six-inch pink pumps that made her thin legs look remarkable. I had no idea how she was able to walk in those heels after drinking all night, but she did it without fault.

Jen was dressed in a sexy little strapless, hot pink party dress with wintergreen pumps. During the winter, Jen was usually so pale. She changed several times before we all agreed that this was the fit for the night. Jen had a live-in boyfriend, but they were basically roommates. Neither of us cared for Robbie and couldn't understand why Jen was still with him. He was such a cheating asshole. Everyone knew he cheated too. After Jen walked in on him fucking someone in her house, she became a different person for a while, but we helped her get back on track quickly.

I didn't know what the fuck Nika was dressed to do. It looked like she was dressed for 5th grade picture day, wearing a modest top and pair of jeans. I couldn't help but wonder if she was trying to hide bruises from that asshole husband of hers under her clothing. I wanted to yank that shirt off and see for myself, but I didn't want to ruin my night since the night was about me.

I was ready for the night of my life. I was relaxed, tipsy, and horny. I dressed better that way. I was extremely colorful. After working out like crazy while deployed, I was ready to show off my smoking body. I purposely packed my clothes the previous night on top. I did not want to dig too deep. I pulled out a purple camisole, to show off my amazingly fit arms and stomach. A pair of turquoise booty shorts to show off my sexy ass and legs, and a very cute pair of peep-toe colorful wedge sandals, which added about 5 inches to my height.

Although sea water isn't good for many, it was good for me. My hair grew an additional 5 inches and fell to the center of my back. My skin was completely clear and glowing. I wrapped my hair up into a messy bun and was accessorized to the "t." We took an abundance of photos before heading to our favorite watering hole.

Already quite tipsy, all inhibitions were out the window. Sasha and I rode with Jen, and Nika drove behind us. I'm sure it was because Jay had her on the clock. But I wasn't going to let that asshole ruin our night.

Surprisingly, none of the girls had been to *Blues* since I left for deployment. The name had now been changed to *Blues and Beds*. We all walked in a little amazed at the new sleek décor. Our old neighborhood bar was now a sheik, sexy mature lounge for the grown and very sexy! The lounge was dark with blue, pink, and purple recess lighting.

There were several black leather couches that lined the walls. The décor on the couches was blue, pink and purple throw pillows. The old corner bar, now circular, sat in the middle of the dance floor with cushioned bar stools. I looked over to where the bar used to be and noticed what I believed to be beds. "A lounge! Surely an odd place for a bed," I thought. But it seemed to compliment the new name and fit in with the new décor and ambiance. Not only was the lounge full of sex appeal, but so were the patrons. And I became excited.

There were so many sexy men and women. I couldn't decide whom to dance with. So, I danced with them all. All night!!! I danced my way to the bar every time I needed a refill. In the midst of all my dancing, I noticed a very attractive guy wearing a hat, wondering how the hell he got in with a hat on. I decided I would ask him tonight once I went home with him. Yep, just like that, I decided to go home with this scrumptious god. He just didn't know it yet. As I was staring at him, he removed his hat. Clearly, he knew I loved a man with a bald head. "Good choice," I whispered to myself. As the night began to come to an end, I walked over to Mr. Bald Guy and informed him that I would be fucking him tonight, at his house, since I hadn't even stepped foot in my house since I had been back.

Nika assured me it was in perfect order just as the pics they sent after setting up my household goods. Since I hadn't actually seen it for myself, I didn't want to take any chances, and damn sure didn't want him to know where I lived, just in case the dick was whack.

Bald Guy smiled and said, "We'll see about that!" and he walked away. I think I was in a state of utter surprise. I giggled. He wanted to play hard to get… Whatever! I was quickly thrust back into reality when I looked at Nika. She was standing on the edge of the dance floor, looking like a lost, scared school girl. Her beautiful face was covered with fright and displeasure. I didn't quite know the details of all the foolishness between Nika and Jay that had transpired since I'd been gone, but I had heard about some of it. "Jay better pray to his funky ass GOD that I never see his black ass again!"

JEN

"Sasha, what time are we leaving? I'm tired," I asked.
"Loosen up Jen, we haven't been out in months, and you haven't been screwed right in months. Relax and let the night just be! All this candy in here, go find something to suck on," Sasha shouted over the music. That was easier said for Sasha. She was gorgeous. Men flocked to her. Sasha could always tell when my mind was on something else. She screamed, "Blah, Jen! Who cares? Stop thinking and dance and try to look sexy doing it."

"I'm going to get another drink. Do you want anything?" I asked.
"Bring me back a shot of tequila," Lace requested, handing me no money, Sasha laughed at the look on my face and asked for a Corona. I headed to the bar, with a little pep in my step, not much as I was completely rhythmless. I wedged my way into a very small opening at the bar next to two skinny half-naked bitches. "Just my luck! These hoes should be where all the men are."
After what felt like an hour, I finally got the bartenders' attention. She smiled and asked, "What can I do you for?"
"That's an accent I hadn't heard before," I thought. "I'll take three shots of tequila and a Corona," I yelled. I felt like I needed a double shot at this point.
"Here you go, my dear," the barmaid said, handing me our drinks.
"How much?" I asked.

"The gentleman at the end of the bar covered it for you," she responded with a wink. I scanned the bar and saw no one familiar to me. I asked the barmaid again, and she waved me off.

As I made my way from the bar, I saw Nika staring off into Neverland with a look of abhorrence on her face. Something was bothering her, but she was being secretive. She had been hiding something, but I was not sure what it was. We talked briefly before the night started about her feelings toward Lace.

She hated her but loved her. Everyone knew how she felt, except Lace. "Here! Drink this," I said as I handed Nika a shot of Tequila. We both took the shot and started dancing. I danced with Nika most of the night with a few interruptions from randoms trying to push up on us.

Nika shot everyone down. She was so faithful to her no-good ass husband, Jay. I loathed him. We all did. Shit, I wasn't any better. I was still with Robbie's stupid ass.

"Jen, I'm heading out. I told Jay I would be home by one. I don't want to upset him," Nika announced.

Unlike Sasha, I stayed silent and hugged Nika goodnight. "Nika, make sure you text me when you get in."

"I'm leaving too!" Sasha yelled.

"Sasha, where are you going?" I questioned.

Sasha mumbled something. I think I just tuned her out and walked away.

I needed to find Lace, so we could hi-tale it out of here. Lace was on the other side of the lounge. She was hugged up next to a sexy lil thang! He was fine! "Lace, let's go. Nika and Sasha have already left," I said as I motioned for her to follow me.

"I'm going home with Bald Guy tonight."

"Lace, you don't even know him, and you're drunk as shit," I reminded her.

"So what, Jen? My God, you act like my mother sometimes. I'll send you a picture of his license plate when I get to the car," Lace slurred.

I wasn't in the mood to go back and forth with Lace. I hugged Lace, told her good night, and to make sure she sends me the picture when she gets to the car.

I headed out of the club after we ended our embrace. I drove home slowly and carefully, considering I was drunk as shit, too. I stumbled in the house in a daze. I poured a glass of water and must have dozed off on the sofa. I was woken by my phone ringing. It was Sasha. She was on the line screaming. I didn't clearly hear what she was saying. Something about Carter and blah blah blah: I was too drunk for this nonsense. But I knew the routine and prepared for one of my best performances.

NIKA

I hated the way Lace looks at me as if she was so much better than me. Judging me with her eyes and always having something negative to say about my husband. "It's not all bad," I tried to tell them, but they didn't believe me. It was Lace's damn fault that I was with Jay anyway. I hoped she felt some guilt when she looks at me with those judgy ass eyes of hers.

"Dance with me, Nika!" Lace screamed into my ear. She was irresistible to everyone. You couldn't help but get excited when she paid you any attention. Except for me, I felt something for Lace, but I wasn't sure what it was. It sometimes felt like a cross between love and hate. Most days, I loved her, but nights when Jay kicked me in my side or stomach, I hated her. My feelings often spilled over or were all mixed together. And when that happened, I found myself having a difficult time enjoying the moment. I wasn't sure if I wanted to "welcome" Lace back home. Sometimes, the sight of her sickened me. Tonight, I'm just feeling blah all together. I probably should have stayed home.

#####

I would have had more fun daydreaming and fantasizing about Lamar. I saw him the other day. We snuck away to a spot near the water. It was only popular in the summertime. We knew no one would be there, and we would practically have the place to ourselves. That was the way I liked it. I wanted him all to myself. He wanted the same but would never admit it. We planned to catch up. It had been almost a week since I last saw him, and I missed him like for real. I did not realize how much I missed him until I saw him. His swag was irrefutable. Although I talked to him practically every day, it was different. I wanted to see him. I needed to be in his presence. That wasn't a good sign.

Of course, we met up during working hours but stayed longer than usual. Sitting, enjoying the presence of each other a little too much, too long and too close. I watched him carefully as I normally did, waiting for him to say what was behind his seductive smile, which he flashed often.

Surely, he would not even acknowledge the thought. Honestly, I didn't really want to know his thoughts. If I knew them, I would have to respond, and I didn't want that. I was glad it was Lamar and no other man. He kept us on the straight and narrow, walking perfectly in sync, ensuring we maintained the balance needed to never fall.

Lamar embraced me as only he can, and I got close as I possible to fill his excitement, still nothing. That was the first time I pondered if he found me attractive. "How does he contain himself?" I wondered. "Because, of course, he finds me attractive, everyone does. I'm not conceited or anything, but I'm very attractive and confident in my looks." Lamar released me from his tightly held embrace, and our lips slightly grazed each other's.

There was an instant spark that shot straight down to my pussy, and it started throbbing. I was panicky and scared. I wanted to kiss him badly. I got anxious and overly excited. That was when I realized I was in love with Lamar. Not a friendship type of love. A high school girl naïve kind of love. The love that gave me butterflies each time I saw him.

That was also the moment I knew our friendship had to end. I didn't want to bring pain and hurt to Lamar, and I didn't want the drama in my own house. I released him that day to save us both from the unthinkable. I didn't speak with haven't spoken to him since and it hurts, badly. I didn't text or see him, and he didn't reach out either. I felt like I was going through my first heartbreak all over again. "It's for the best," I kept telling myself.

The worst part about it is I couldn't talk about my pain with anyone, not even him. I didn't know I could still feel love like this again. I was excited about him, every inch of him. I often tried to find things I disliked about him to push myself away from him, but I came up empty every time.

#####

"Drink this," Jen said, shoving a shot of tequila in my face. We took shot after shot and danced all night long. I tried to dance Lamar out of my thoughts, but the alcohol just made the thoughts more ubiquitous. I danced so long and so hard that I didn't notice the time. I told Jay I would be home by one. "He is probably going to be pissed."

"Jen!" I screamed over the music, but she didn't hear me. She was in her own little world of drunkenness. "Jen!" I screamed again as I tapped her shoulder, "I'm leaving. I told Jay I would be back by 1:00 a.m."

"Fuck him!" Sasha yelled with force and energy from behind Jen, while grinding on some random sailor. I knew he was a sailor by his bowl cut and whack style.

"Navy boys all dressed out of style, trying to bring back the last best thing from their hometown," I chuckled to myself, thinking about that. I rolled my eyes at Sasha, but she had just found Tony. I wasn't sure she even noticed me. I hugged Sasha and Jen. I looked around for Lace to say goodnight and spotted her on the other side of the lounge. She was looking extremely friendly with some random, not sailor random, though—maybe a local random, or a sailor's husband random. "Who knows? You can never know with Lace. I'm sure we'll hear all about it in the morning."

I decided to let Lace enjoy herself since she had our entire weekend planned out. I said my final goodnights and walked out of the club toward my car. I spotted the fake ass cops, standing outside, looking for someone to harass. The seven cities had the worst fucking cops. It was like their entire goal in life was to harass military folk. I swear, they got a kick out it! "I can't wait to be transferred out of Norfolk," I thought as I rushed toward my car.

I made it to my car without being harassed by the cops. My head began to spin, and I began to feel a little sick as I put my key in the door. I sat in the driver seat contemplating driving home, taking a cab, or calling Lamar to come and pick me up. Lamar didn't drink and hated it when I drank and drove. I had never called him this time of night. I didn't usually call him at all. We never talked on the phone. We only sent text messages or talked in person. I dismissed the thought as I concluded I would be using this as an excuse to see him after our last outing. "It's not a good idea to be around him drunk," I thought.

When we were out together, I never have more than two drinks. Most times, I didn't drink at all. I didn't want to take the chance of saying or doing anything else to jeopardize our friendship. I was hoping we could eventually recover from our last brush up. I didn't quite know how to approach it, but I was hoping he did. I opted to drive. I started the car and began my journey home. I reached for my cell and tried calling Jay to tell him I was on my way, but he didn't answer. "I sure hope he's sleep; I'm just not up for his bullshit tonight."

SASHA

"I'm leaving with Tony. I'll call you in the a.m.," I screamed to Jen. "Jen acts like she's our mother. She needs someone to do, so she can stay out of my business."

"She just worries about you Sasha, we all do," said Nika;

"I'm leaving now too. Be careful! And seriously, call me in the a.m., bitch!"

"I will," I sighed, responding to Nika.

Tony and I have the most amazing fuck sessions and tonight will be no different. He was nothing like Carter, bitch ass. I met Tony three months About a month after Carter and Sonya's big porn reveal. I was at

Military Circle Mall, working in the boutique. Tony was nothing like those military boys! He walked into my store while I was dressing a manikin and stood uncomfortably close to me. I normally wouldn't let a man get that close to me, being married and all, but after what Carter did, I was here for all the fuckery. I was all the way open for new opportunities now. It was the only way I knew how to get over Carter.

Tony drove down to the Best Western Plus near the beach to get us a room for the night. I sat in the car while Tony went to check us in. His phone rang like crazy all night. I'm sure it was his nasty ass baby mama. I looked at his phone to see 33 missed calls from "BM."

Without even thinking, I pulled my shorts to the side, spread my legs, and snapped a picture of my perfectly shaven pussy. I went to the call log and found "BM's" number, and I attached the picture I just took.

Just for clarity, I added the caption, "He's a little occupied tonight, hunty," and immediately hit send. I smiled at my mischievous behavior and instantly deleted the pic and text. I didn't want Tony to see it. I was sure he would find out soon, but I was not ready for him to find out before I got mine. I found his power button and turned his phone off so there would be no more interruptions. "There's absolutely no need to ruin my night!"

Tony came walking back to the car from the lobby of the hotel. He came to the passenger side, where I was sitting and opened the door. "Check in complete!" he said as a smile graced his face.

"What are you smiling at?" I asked sweetly.

"You," he replied. I had my legs spread wide open across his dashboard, pleasuring myself.

"I guess you just couldn't wait for me?" I ignored him and continued in my self-play. He watched raptly until I released gently on his passenger seat, right where his BM sat. Tony wouldn't let me fix myself. He wanted me to walk in just as I was. I wore no underwear and had removed my shorts in the car to guarantee I got into the best position for self-play. I indulged. I wasn't ashamed of my body.

We entered a room on the first floor. I don't even know if the door was closed before I was shoved onto the bed and his tongue in my ass—his tongue going in and out my ass while fingering my pussy made my secretions overflow. His extensive tongue game made it easy for his dick to slide in. His raw shaft in my ass excited me and intensified with every thrust. This time was a little different, though he controlled the situation. My ass was tilted up as Tony held my legs in the air. He rammed his hard shaft into my ass until we finally exploded together. We both fell onto the bed and lay infused.

Tony gazed into my eyes, intimately. I felt him coming in closer. I puckered my lips as I prepared for a kiss. He reached over me and handed me my phone instead. I didn't realize it was ringing; I was so engaged in the moment. I answered without looking at the caller ID.

"Where the fuck are you, Sasha?" yelled Carter.

I looked at the phone in shock, "Why are you yelling?" I screamed.

"I am at Jen's house. I drank too much and couldn't drive home," I responded.

"Really, Sasha? Well, when you're done sobering up, have Tony call home. The picture of your legs spread and pussy showing in the front seat of his car has his baby mama in an uproar," Carter screamed from the other end of the phone.

"Carter, I have no idea what you are talking about. I'm at Jen's house. I have been here since we left the lounge. If you don't believe me, just drive over here," I said as I hung up the phone. Reality hit quickly.

Why the fuck did I tell him I was at Jen's? I jumped up and into the shower. I rinsed all the important body parts. Tony ran out to the car to get my shorts. I was out of the shower by the time he came back in. I decided it would be quicker to air dry, I jumped in my clothes, and we headed to Jen's. Tony was driving like a bat out of hell. I called Jen on the way there and told her the situation.

We decided I would come in through the front door since everybody used the back. I'd sneak into Alicia's room, out of sight of Robbie.

Carter was coming from my house, which was about 40 minutes north of Jen's house. I was coming from the Best Western Plus, which was about 25 minutes south. I should beat him there, but just in case I didn't, Jen knew how to stall. We usually covered for each other all the time. Lately, it had become second nature.

Coming through the front door, I heard Jen talking to someone. I wondered how the fuck Carter beat me here. I made my way to Alicia's room and lay in the extra bed. I softly pretended to snore, like I often did when I was drunk. Seconds later, Carter walked his dumb ass in.

We started counseling shortly after Carter and Sonya's big porn reveal—three times a week. "A waste of fucking time, if you ask me!" I even entertained trivial and bombastic family counseling sessions. Sonya, my parents, and Carter all attended blissfully. As if some deep-seated issues would be resolved. I was over all that shit. I had no desire to save my marriage at all. I did, however, want to maintain my lifestyle until I could afford it on my own.

I worked a meaningless boutique job with minimum pay and

responsibilities. I had access to the newest sexiest clothing and freshest styles, half off, of course, if not free. I was able to drop off and pick up my boys to and from school. I drove a gray Maserati and had no idea of the monthly payment. Since the affair, I had grown a deep hatred for Carter and Sonya. I could barely stomach them. Carter and I were not in good terms, by any means, but he believed we were getting there. I played along because I loved my life, and my boys loved their dad. I started saving all my paychecks. "Once I have enough money stashed, it's over between us."

Carter looked in on me, lying across the bed and decided to leave me there to sleep my drunkenness off.

CHAPTER 9
NIKA

I made it home and sat in the car for a while, trying to gather my thoughts. I said a silent prayer to thank God for allowing me to make it home. As I was praying, I became extremely nauseous. I knew it was time to go inside and lay my head down! I stumbled my drunk ass out of my car to the front door.

I somehow managed to get my key in the lock after struggling for what seemed like forever. The door swung open, and I jumped, thinking it was Jay, but it was just the wind…whew! "Thank God," I whispered.

I started walking up the stairs into my house. Walking, stumbling, it was all the same thing that time of the morning. When I reached the top step, I saw bloodshot-eyed, angry, dark Jay standing in front of me, huffing and puffing. He looked just like the monster he had become. During that thought, I felt a sting across my face. Jay hit me so hard that I flew back down to the first step.

"Oh, my God!" was all I could say. "So, tonight is the night he's going to kill me." I felt it in my soul. I hit my head on the door as I was flung down the stairs and was dazed. I tried to shake it off and reach for the doorknob. If I was going to survive, I had to escape.

I looked back to see how much space was between us, and as I turned, I saw Jay jump into the air like a crazy maniac over the steps. He landed right on top of me—all 236 pounds—crushing my 115-body frame. I started crying and fighting. I was swinging and kicking, but I was no match for him. He grabbed me by my hair and threw my head into the wall. My head bounced back into his grip.

He tightened his grip around my hair as if he was grasping a rope and dragged me back up the stairs. I looked up, and through my eyes, all I saw was blood, but I had no idea where it was coming from. I didn't feel pain or any cut. All I felt was fear. I looked into Jay's eyes through the blood streaming down my face and saw a pure devil. It was like he was a different person. I was searching his face for mercy, when I saw him reach over to the sage corner table near the top of the steps and pick up a ceramic lamp my mother gave us as a gift. I didn't even have time to think before he broke it across my head. The lamp shattered into pieces. I was screaming and fighting as hard as I could, but I was weak and sick and tired. All these thoughts rushed through me as Jay punched me repeatedly.

There was a pause; I think he's trying to regain his strength. With that pause, I took off, running toward the kitchen. It was the adrenaline at this point. I was fighting and running off fumes. "You stupid bitch!" Jay yelled as he grabbed me by my hair, "You can't run from me, bitch!"

With a fist full of my hair, Jay slammed me onto the floor, and I started to feel his foot piercing my side as he kicked me continually. He paused…I mustered up some energy, stood up, and ran again toward the kitchen. I was trying everything to get away from him, but he kept overpowering me. This time, he grabbed me by my hair with so much force that he yanked a patch from my head by the roots. With every pause, I ran. With every run, he was angered more than the last. It didn't matter; I kept trying to get to the kitchen. I didn't have a plan; I just didn't want to go out without a fight.

I cried, and I cried, and I yelled, "Stop, Jay! Stop it! Leave me alone. You're hurting me." I don't know why I wasted my breath; he didn't care that he was hurting me; he never cared when he hurt me.

I was screaming and crying. Jay punched me in my face over and over until I stopped fighting; until I stopped crying. Fear and drunkenness had crippled me. I looked up at Jay, hoping he would stop when he saw my blood-soaked face, but no such luck. I saw his hands moving toward my neck through my swollen eyes. Jay began chocking me as he ripped my jeans off and shoved his dick in me with vigor. He pumped and pumped harder and harder, each time tightening the grip of his hands around my neck. It's true, you know, your entire life really does flash before your eyes.

I saw every memorable moment, every joy, and every pain, come rushing into my thoughts. The worst part about it is, this wasn't Jay's first time beating me, but I couldn't help but think it would be his last. I felt death creeping in—complete blackness. I lost consciousness.

It's dark, and I'm cold. I can't see. My eyes feel like they're glued shut. I try to search the area with my hands to see where I am, but I can't feel anything. I don't think my hands moved either. I hear something. It sounds familiar to me. It's crying I hear. It's it me crying? Can someone see me?" I try to speak to get the attention of whoever is near, but I can't. My mouth is full of liquid. Thick liquid. It tastes like metal, maybe blood. I feel myself choking.

The sound is getting closer. It sounds like DD. I tried again to open my mouth to ask for help but it's too much blood and pain. I can't see her, but I know it's her. I hear her talking. "Who is she talking to? Oh God, I hope Jay is not here." Then I listen intently. "She's on the phone," I think. She's calling for help!" "My mommy is hurt. She's on the kitchen floor. She's bleeding, and I don't think she's breathing," DD says. "Oh, my

God, am I dead? Am I not breathing?"

Questions rush through my brain as I lay there motionless. I began to cry or, I think, I'm crying. I'm not crying for my own pain. I'm crying for the pain of my daughter. "Why did I do this to her? Why would I stay with this man and allow her to see me like this? Why would I risk the chance of DD having to bury her mother? I'm stupid; that's why." I cry more, I think. I feel something—little hands. They're DD's hands. I hear her cries. She's lying next to me now.

I feel her head on my chest. "I must be alive, if I can feel her," I thought. I hear something. I attempted to open my eyes but still nothing. In the same moment that I understood what I was feeling; she was gone. Just that quick the feeling is gone. "Was I dreaming? Am I dead? Or did someone lift her off me? Please, God, don't let it be Jay coming back to finish me off," I panic. There's a lot of movements around me: a lot of yelling. I can't make anything out. There's pushing and shoving. My head is being moved to the left—something is in my mouth. "A finger? I think. I don't know what's happening. Then, blackness, and I lose consciousness.

LACE

I don't think we made it past his front door before I was pinned to a wall, and his face was between my thighs. I had no idea what he was doing down there, but it caused me an immediate release. Moments later, there was a double release, and it was good. "This random is trying to make the team," I thought. He was so good I started begging for his dick. At that point, I hadn't seen it. I didn't even know what he was working with, but it had to be something amazing, I decided.

In the middle of my thoughts, he picked me up and carried me to the bedroom. He threw me onto the bed. I landed on my back, and he buried his head in my pussy again. I moaned and screamed from the satisfaction, cumming again. I felt cum oozing out of my pussy down my thighs onto his bed.

Then he flipped me over with one single hand movement onto my stomach. "He is strong," I thought to myself. Then he flipped me again. "What's with him and these damn flips?" This time the flip was followed by straight pressure entering my body. He held both my legs with one hand a little off to the side.

All I could see were my colorful wedges as he penetrated me long and hard repeatedly. I remember screaming several times before being told to shut the fuck up!

"You wanted to fuck, right? Now take this monster," he

demanded.

And a monster it was! It was long and thick. I still hadn't seen it, but I could only imagine its beauty. He finally released himself on my stomach. I was so drunk and so relaxed; I was ready for sleep.

Mr. Bald Guy exhausted as hell, looked at me and motioned for me to pleasure him, after such great treatment. I conceded. Not to brag, but I did my best work under the influence of heavy liquor.

I woke up the next morning with a horrible headache. I blinked a couple of times, trying to find my bearings. "Where the hell am I?" A few minutes passed before I noticed this gorgeous silhouette out of the corner of my eye. The silhouette entered the room, and there stood a gorgeous naked man. He had a smile that filled the room.

"Who the fuck are you, and where am I?" I asked.

"According to how you introduced me to your friends last night, I believe my name is Bald Guy," he responded with a smile.

From the look on my face, he could see I was still at a loss for words. "We met last night," he continued, "at Blues and Beds, on the beach." I twisted my lip upward as I often do when I am confused. I began to see the frustration on his face as he continued.

"You walked up to me, smiled quite innocently, and told me you were going to fuck me silly." After an awkward silence, laughter filled the air. The laugher made my head hurt worst. He could see I was in pain.

"Take this," he demanded as he shoved a BC packet in my face.

"Do you have any beer?" I asked sheepishly. "I may have a beer or two," he responded. He left the room to retrieve my beverage. As he walked away, I couldn't help but stare. He had the most amazing ass. He must have felt me staring. He didn't say a word when he returned to the bedroom. He grabbed my legs, pushed them as far apart as they could go, and plunged right in. I remembered him now, I wanted to yell! He ravished my body in the morning glow, allowing me to release. It felt good. I hadn't been fucked like that since before deployment, actually since Marcus, but Mr. Bald Guy surely made up for all the randoms that helped me to pass the time.

My moans were interrupted by the constant ringing of my phone. I ignored it, but it seemed to be a distraction to my new friend.

"I think your friends maybe a little concerned about you. Give them a call," he motioned.

"Oh, blah," I said as I picked up the phone. I picked up the phone only to notice 16 missed calls from Jen and 12 from Sasha. Sasha called last, so I called her back immediately.

"What the hell are you doing?" Sasha yelled into the phone when she answered.

"OMG! What's up? Who died?" I responded.

"What bitch! Shut the hell up with your smart remarks!" Sasha snapped back.

"What smart remarks? You've been blowing my phone up so obviously someone must have died!" I said in a raised tone.

"Whatever!" Sasha responded. "Jen and I just got to the hospital. Meet us at Portsmouth; something happened to Nika," she said in an aggravated tone.

"Something like what, Sasha?" I asked.

"I don't know, Lace. Her mom called and told us to get here ASAP. You didn't answer, so Jen and I came as quickly as we could," Sasha responded as she hung up.

"Hello…Sasha?" Fuck! She hung up on me.

Bald Guy looked at me puzzled and asked: "What's wrong? Is there something I can do?"

"That was Sasha. My friend Nika is in the hospital. Can you drive me to Portsmouth Naval?" I asked.

"Of course!" Bald Guy responded. I felt myself getting angry, knowing I couldn't get any answers until I arrived, and I tried calming myself down.

"Do you mind if I take a quick shower?" I asked. "And I'm going to need some sweatpants and a sweatshirt," I demanded. Bald Guy laughed and indulged my every command. Once I was cleaned up and dressed in my new gear, we headed to the hospital. I took my beer to go to help calm my nerves. We didn't speak much because I had to stay sane. Bald Guy pulled up to the front to drop me off. I leaned over and kissed him long and hard.

As I opened the door to exit the car, I exclaimed, "Nice meeting you! Hope to run into you again soon."

Bald Guy put his car in park and jumped out after me. "Wait! Can I have your number or at least your name?" he asked.

I smiled, "That's not how a one-night stand works," I said.

"Okay, but what about my clothes? Can I at least get your number? That's one of my favorite sets, and I would love to have them back," he said. I smiled and yelled out my number as I walked away. "He doesn't need my name just to get his clothes back," I thought.

I heard whispers and cries. I opened my eyes, and this time, I could see, not a lot, but enough to make out what was around me. I looked right into the eyes of my mother. Then I saw Sasha and Jen. DD was crawled up next to me on the bed. I was looking around, confused. I had no idea where I was. I paused for a minute and realized I was in the hospital.

It was Portsmouth Naval Hospital. There were tubes in my nose and a butterfly needle in my arm for IV. I looked over to the IV stand, and there were three bags hanging. A large bag for fluid, I'm sure, and two smaller bags. "But what happened to me? Why am I here?" Jen must have seen my confusion. She and my mom smiled and touched me gently, without speaking. They'd been crying. Their eyes were bloodshot red. Jen's face looked puffy. My mom looked drained. Sasha was on the phone, whispering to someone, probably Lace. My voice was only a whisper.

My mouth was dry. I could barely get words out. "What happened?" I whispered. As soon as those words left my lips, Lace walked in, and she was ANGRY!

"What the fuck happened? Who did this? Was it that motherfucking Jay?" Lace yelled.

"Calm down! Nika doesn't need you all wound up right now," Jen said.

"Fuck that!" Lace screamed. When Lace gets mad, watch out, world! Jen looked at me as if she was searching for answers. Maybe she was searching for words. She looked distant and perplexed.

"Nika," she spoke softly. "Do you remember anything from last night?" Jen asked.

"No. Can you tell me?" I asked.

My mom began to cry.

Lace's face was fuming with anger. "Get off the fucking phone, Sasha!" Lace yelled. She then snarled at Jen, "Are you going to fucking tell her or what?"

Jen took a deep breath and said, "Short version: you were beaten, raped, and left for dead. DD found you in the kitchen clinging to life near the stove. She was brave. She picked up the phone and dialed 911. She was clutched to your side when help arrived. Paramedics had to pull her away from you. She cried herself to sleep while you were in surgery."

"Surgery?" I whispered.

"Yes, surgery. But you're okay now. The doctors said you'd make a full recovery," Jen concluded.

Tears filled up in my eyes. I cried. My mother cried. Jen cried. Sasha, finally off the phone, cried, but not Lace. She didn't cry. Her cries were reserved for heartbreaks only. She began to pace the floor.

My mother leaned in and cradled me until I finally stopped crying. That was the first time my mother had ever comforted me through my pain. She held me for what felt like forever. She slowly let me go, laying me back on my pillow.

Lace got right in my face and said, "You're not going back to that motherfucker, and I mean it." She looked at Jen and Sasha, who were both trying to gain their composure and said, "We should fucking kill him!"

Jen looked at Lace and shook her head. "Lace, let's focus on Nika's recovery. We can discuss that later," Jen said.

"Fuck you and fuck that!" Lace screamed. "I'm sick of focusing on her recovery. How many more times are we going to focus on her recovery before we're burying our fucking friend?" Lace's words were acidulous. They pierced a part of me that wasn't already bruised, and I cried. Hysterically. Lace was right, though. "How many more times will he beat me and leave me for dead? This had to be it. But I said that the last time. Do I mean it now that everyone knows?" Honestly, they probably all knew before and just let me live in my lies.

LACE

"Nika, have you spoken to the cops. Did you tell them it was Jay that did this?" I asked.

"Lace, she doesn't remember, she doesn't even know it was Jay," Jen stated.

"Shut the fuck up, Jen. Who else is going to do this? You sound so fucking stupid," I yelled.

"No. I haven't spoken to the cops," Nika responded.

"They did do a rape kit," Ms. Rogers, Nika's mom, responded.

"Good! They'll catch the bastard," I said.

"Lace, those tests take months to come back. Unless Nika can remember, there will be no arrest anytime soon," Sasha chimed in.

I couldn't believe it. I felt like I was the only one in the room angry. I had fucking questions. "What do you mean months? How many months? This bastard will roam free while we wait on test results? He will kill her, don't you all know that? We need a plan to protect our friend," I said all at once. I think I was babbling at that point.

"Lace, let's talk about this later. Everyone's emotions are high right now. We're probably all still drunk from last night. We need to regroup and have a civil conversation later," Sasha suggested. But it was something about the way Sasha spoke those words that made me nervous. It gave me the sense that something was in motion.

Sasha's phone rang, and she went to the corner to whisper to someone. I heard her give out a code, an entry code. It sounded very analogous to the entry code to my house.

"Sasha, who are you talking too?" I asked.

Sasha raised her finger to her lips and motioned for me to be silent. She was eerily calm. First, I was nervous, but now I was excited. I looked over at Jen, and she gave me a slight grin. I was not exactly sure what was going on. They've had a few more hours to process this, and if they could be calm, I could too.

We sat with Nika most of the day throughout the early evening. I thought of several different ways to castigate Jay for the pain and suffering he caused my friend. I wasn't the only one, though. We were friends for a reason. We all thought and acted so much alike. I could see on Jen's and Sasha's faces that they too wanted to punish him. Severely! We all wanted him dead. We wanted to kill him. I could see their minds were racing. Sasha took several secretive calls. She would never say who they were. We didn't talk about what we wanted to do to Jay; we all just thought it, simultaneously.

"Nika, we're about to head out. We'll take turns checking on you," Sasha explained. Ms. Rogers packed up with DD at the same time.

"Sasha, I need a ride home," I said.

"I know. We're all heading to your house, anyway," Sasha responded. We said our final good nights to Nika, Ms. Rogers and DD and started heading out. As we were walking down the hall to catch the elevator, I was busy on my phone and was startled by a unison, "Oh shit!" from both Sasha and Jen.

They both looked at me with pity as I looked past them and noticed a godly figure of perfection. He stopped right in from of me and went in for an instant hug. Sasha moved over to stand in between us.

"Lacey, how have you been?" he asked.

I was silent. I couldn't speak. I didn't know what or how to say anything. I was stuck. My eyes swelled up with tears. In my head, I screamed, "WHY THE FUCK ARE YOU CRYING?" Jen and Sasha both saw the tears start to roll down my cheeks.

"Not today, Lacey! Not to fucking day!" Sasha yelled as she grabbed my left hand, and Jen grabbed my right. They motioned for me to keep walking. I wanted to stay there in that moment. I had questions, dammit, but each time I tried, they tightened their grips. We walked hand in hand into the elevator. Sasha hit the button for the first floor. The doors opened, and we walked hand in hand out of the hospital. I didn't look back. I wanted to. I desperately wanted to, but I didn't.

It seemed like it took us forever to make it to Jen's car. Once I got inside the car on the back-passenger side, I screamed. I bellowed a gut-wrenching sound and cried. I hit the seat several times as the crying got worse. I was incensed. Jen and Sasha said nothing. They knew the pain I was feeling all too well and allowed my tears to flow without judgment. They got me over my initial heartbreak two years ago, and now it was back front and center. They made several trips to Maryland while I was stationed there to get me through plenty of lonely recovering heartbroken nights.

We pulled up to my driveway. I was still in full-blown tears, trying to gather myself. My mind was still on that godly perfection. My house sat right at the end of Sir Meliot Drive. I barely remembered what it looked like, honestly. I found and closed on the house so quickly, and then I was gone. It all happened so fast. The experience which was supposed to be fun and exciting was a fading memory. Sasha opened the front door to my modest 3-bedroom two-bath home. I stopped short of entering and asked, "Why does it still hurt so badly?" to no one in particular.

Neither Sasha nor Jen responded. They simply ushered me into the house. I walked through the house noticing nothing and went down the hall to my bedroom. I fell on the bed and began to cry. A part of me wasn't sure why I was crying. I was convinced I didn't still love Marcus. I had been under, and on top of so many randoms, there was no way I still had any love for him. I cried, and I cried until I finally drifted off to sleep.

My eyes flickered open, and I saw Sasha on the side of me and felt Jen on the other. My mind started racing. Jen and Sasha spoke before Marcus did. "How did they know that was Marcus?" They both said something before I even noticed him. "We all know how small the Navy is, could they have known him and didn't tell me? Would they watch me suffer and not say anything? I need to get to the hospital and talk to Nika. These two would hide the truth, but Nika wouldn't. She's too vulnerable to hide anything from me at this point. Would I be wrong to question her in her current state?" I wondered.

SASHA

Jen and I didn't say a single word to each other or to Lace on the way to her house. We allowed Lace to cry, scream, and yell. The pain and love she still carried for Marcus were real. We wanted to discuss our plans concerning Jay with her, but she was in no shape and too distracted. She went to her room, crawled into her bed, and fell asleep, still crying.

A part of me hoped she would remain distracted. We surely did not want her to find out we knew where Marcus was the entire time she'd struggled to get over him. We had all seen pictures of Marcus but hadn't physically met him until almost a year after he left Lace hanging high and dry.

Jen and I had already decided to kill Jay, and we just needed Lace on board. We protected one another by any means necessary. We did the same for Jen when Axel started taking her down that rocky path of drug addiction. We didn't go to the same extreme to protect Lace from Marcus when Marcus tried to get in touch with Lace a year and a half ago. But we did purposely keep him away from her.

Marcus arrived at Norfolk three days after leaving Pensacola in 2001 and coincidently was stationed with Carter. Soon as he arrived at Norfolk, his boat deployed. He claimed that was the reason he hadn't contacted Lace when he left Pensacola. We knew that wasn't true. And even if it was true, it had nothing to do with him sneaking out like a thief in the night without even saying goodbye. Carter and Marcus were deployed for over seven months. They worked in the same shop and became good friends during the deployment.

When Carter's boat returned from deployment, some of the other wives and I had planned a mega welcome home party. This was back when I loved Carter. I invited Lace, Jen, and Nika, because we always did everything together. Lace declined, as she was in no shape to take the drive down from Maryland. Almost a year after, she was still in her Marcus funk.

The husbands invited damn near the entire boat to the welcome home party. One of the other couples hosted at their house since their home was massive. Their home also had plenty of land and an Olympic size swimming pool. So many people showed up for the party that it felt more like a welcome home, block party.

The weather was perfect and complemented the outdoor gathering. Jen and Nika met me there. Once the party began to wind down, we found our way to a card table. We stayed at the spades table, kicking ass and taking names. Nika and I were partners, and Jen played with some random. We were having a great time when Marcus recognized Jen from some photos Lace had shared with him. Marcus walked up to the table and addressed Jen, "You don't know me, but my name is Marcus, I'm a friend of Lace."

It was as if the entire world stopped moving. Nika, Jen, and I made immediate eye contact. Without even looking up, Nika asked, "And what the fuck do you want, asshole?" Marcus was taken aback. He clearly didn't know that we knew all about his trifling ass. Marcus explained his actions in an attempt to get Lace's number. Although she had given it to him during their time in Pensacola, he had gotten a new phone and lost all his contacts. I took that as a sign that it wasn't important enough for him to treasure. We refused to give Marcus the number. Although we did consider it, bearing in mind the pain he had already caused, we decided against it. I also made Carter promise to stay fucking out of it.

I had to constantly remind Carter, not to invite Marcus around when Lace was there. Marcus and Carter had become good friends. It had gotten difficult to keep him away. We all liked Marcus a lot, too, we genuinely enjoyed having him around and hung out with him as often as we could, but we couldn't take the chance of him hurting Lace again. And now seeing how Lace still cried for him damn near four years later, I knew we made the best decision for our friend.

CHAPTER 10
NIKA

I was awoken by the sun, brightly shining through the blinds. Fresh flowers by my bedside, yellow roses. A sign of friendship. "The girls must have had them delivered," I thought. I slightly turned my head and realized I wasn't alone. Lamar sat on the chair to the left side of my hospital bed. He didn't notice I was awake. I watched him intently until he finally noticed. "Good morning, Nika," he spoke softly and slowly. He stood up and walked to the side of my bed. He grabbed my hand and caressed it slowly. "This is the first time Lamar has ever initiated signs of affection," I thought. My body didn't react. It was in so much pain. My heart leaped, though.

Lamar placed my hand down and pulled the chair he sat on close to my bed. He sat down and grabbed my hand again. This time, he put it close to his face—rubbing it against his smooth skin, he lands it on his lips and gently kisses it. He had never done that before, though we had held hands before—plenty of times.

The first time we held hands, we were at Lace's house was early fall while we were unpacking and setting up Lace's house. Sasha and Jen weren't there. Lamar and I snuck away from the office and agreed to meet at Lace's. I told him I needed his muscle to rearrange some furniture and hang some pictures on the wall. He knew it was just another excuse I used for us to spend alone time together. I loved spending time with Lamar, and he always agreed to my request. It didn't matter how out the way they were.

Lace's house was somewhat secluded, a perfect location for one of our outings. In route, Lamar stopped by our favorite sandwich shop, Sam's Texas Sub Shop, and ordered our favorite subs. We always ordered the same sandwiches and would split the sandwich in half and share them. Lamar stopped by the liquor store and grabbed my favorite wine, too. I usually enjoyed a glass of wine with every meal, sometimes I felt a little weird about drinking alone, but I would enjoy my wine none the less.

Lamar pulled up to Lace's house while I sat on the porch, taking in the neighborhood, anxiously awaiting his arrival. We greeted each other with a sensual, but platonic hug as we always did. He held me closer than usual, probably to feel my breast against his chest. He often held me tighter on days I didn't wear a bra.

We ended our embrace and walked in through the front door. I gave Lamar a tour around Lace's house, which had been put together very well, or so I thought. We walked through the living into the dining room and out the patio door. A large wood deck was attached. "This is beautiful," Lamar said as he sat the bags down on the built-in wooden benches.

"We're heading to the back, behind the gates. We can sit and eat out there. There are chairs out for us already," I announced.

Lamar followed me to the back, and I unlatched the gate. He handed me the bags he held and pushed the gate open—just enough for us to pass through. The area was wooded with a lot of fallen trees. There was a slight path. I could see a reflection of the sun glistening off the lake.

I led us to two chairs and a cooler that sat on the flattest part of the land directly in front of the water. The small roller cooler sat in the middle of the chairs. The atmosphere was serene. We sat down and got comfortable. Lamar handed me the sandwich of which the sandwich shop had already swamped the halves. As I unwrapped my sandwich, Lamar opened my bottle of wine with the corkscrew that sat on top of the cooler. In my chair cup holder sat a portable wine glass. In Lamar's cup holder sat a Coke. I usually frowned at Lamar when he drank soda, but occasionally, I would allow him to indulge without judgment. Lamar poured me a glass of wine all the way to the top just as I liked it. We sat quietly and ate our sandwiches and enjoyed our beverages of choice.

When we were done eating, without looking, I reached out my hand to thank him for lunch, and Lamar grabbed it. I wasn't expecting that, but I surely wasn't about to let go. I interlocked my fingers with his, and we held hands for the first time. We sat there holding hands, talking about everything with nothing in between.

#####

He spoke softly, almost in a whisper. "You scared me, Nika. I've missed you." That was all he said. He sat with me, never letting go of my hand. I should have told him what happened, but I simply texted him the hospital room number, and he came immediately, never asking what happened. He never would. He always waited for me to share because he knew I couldn't resist sharing parts of my life with him. Kind of cocky, if you think about it, and of course, he was right: I'd let him in when the time was right.

Lace walked in as Lamar and I stared at each other in silence, though we both wanted to say a lot. I assumed particularly about how we felt for each other. Maybe we even loved each other. But we would never be so bold. So, we stared, knowing what the other thought and felt, yet too afraid to express any of it. Lace glanced around the room, then from me to Lamar.

She took note that Lamar was holding my hand in his. "Who's this lame?" Lace asked.

Lamar smiled. Never intimated or offended by others' comments. Still smiling, he stood, reached out his right hand, still holding my hand with his left, and introduced himself, "Hi, I'm Lamar, a work friend of Nika's."

Lace shook his hand and glanced down at him, still holding my hand. "You two look really friendly and comfortable," Lace said. Lace was very protective of all her friends. "You're married, I see," Lace continued. Lamar smiled, "I am," he responded.

"Does your wife know you're here?" Lace asked.

Lamar and I answered in unison, "It's working hours."

We looked at each other and laughed. Hysterically.

Lace didn't get it. No one got our inside jokes. If it was during working hours, our friendship was acceptable in our eyes. The problem with that is, it was not working hours. It was Sunday. Although we had never crossed any lines that would indicate unfaithfulness, we lied to ourselves often to make ourselves feel better about our friendship. "I'll let you spend time with…" Lamar paused, waiting for Lace to provide her with a name.

Instead, Lace rolled her eyes in true Lace fashion from deep within her soul and waved him off. "That's Lace," I said, salvaging her rudeness.

"Lacey, it's great to finally meet you," he said. Everyone called her Lace, but Lamar liked her full name. We once jokingly talked about fostering a child together. Forging paperwork for our spouses and sharing the child between both families.

"If it's a girl, we'll name her after Lacey," Lamar said.

Lace didn't like the fact that Lamar knew her, and she had never heard of him. "I wish I could say the same," she snarled.

Lamar smiled and glanced at me, noting Lace's comment was toward me. Lamar let go of my hand and moved his hand to my forehead. He moved a few strands of my hair, leaned down, and kissed me gently where the hairs once were. "I'll see you soon," he whispered.

Lace watched Lamar closely as he walked out of the hospital room and noted: "He's a Zaddy, for real." I laughed.

"He's not that much older than us, Lace; but he is off-limits," I responded.

"Protective of our work friend, aren't we?" Lace responded while using air quotes. I ignored Lace's remark, but that didn't stop her from prying.

"Have you fucked him?" she asked abruptly.

"Oh, my God! Lace? You know I would never cheat on Jay!" I said.

"Fuck Jay!" Lace yelled. Sasha and Jen walked in just in time to co-sign Lace's remarks.

I was thankful. I'd rather them talk about Jay than Lamar. I didn't want them to know about Lamar. He was my friend, and I didn't want to share him with them or anyone else for that matter. It was bad enough I had to share him with his family. Sasha and Jen walked over, and both kissed me on my cheek.

Lace smiled, walked over behind them, and imitated the exact moves Lamar had previously made.

"What the hell is wrong with you, Lace?" Jen asked.

Lace laughed and said, "That's what Nika's work friend just did," again using stupid air quotes.

"What work friend? We know all her friends?" Jen asked.

"You ever heard of a Lamar?" Lace asked as she sashayed across the room. "No!" Sasha and Jen both responded.

Lace continued, "Oh, yes. He was just here. He's married, but he can get it; however, Nika just put him on the cannot-fuck list." Sasha looked at me and smiled, "Work friend my ass!" she said as they all started to laugh. The do-not-fuck list is reserved for real loves, like Carter, Marcus and now apparently Lamar. I did not laugh as my eyes became focused on the figure standing in the doorway.

JEN

The sound of Jay's voice abruptly stopped our laugher. He stood at the doorway of Nika's hospital room. I became enraged. "Call the fucking cops," I yelled. I ran right up in Jay's face, "Get the fuck out!" I said. Jay looked at me and wanted to move me out of the way. I shoved him, pushing him into the nurse's station.

Sasha and Lace ran over to where I stood. "Don't you ever put your hands on me again," I screamed. Jay stood up and charged at me. He didn't consider that he had an unfair advantage until he got right in my face. He looked at the three of us and demanded we move out his way. Nika silly ass begged us to move. I was disgusted. I was so over her shit. We moved. I walked back to Nika's bedside as Jay walked to the other side.

Jay leaned down and kissed her. I wanted to throw up. "Nika, you don't have to tolerate this. You're better than this. You don't have to be his punching bag. You can have him arrested," I said without taking a breath in-between.

Jay ignored me and demanded that Nika tell us he had done nothing wrong. She did just as she was instructed with tears in her eyes.

I knelt close to my friend and begged her to be strong. "It wasn't him," Nika said. Jay smiled and announced he was on duty and had nothing to do with the attack. Lace was so angry; she launched at Jay.

Jay moved back and laughed. As Jay was laughing, I couldn't help myself. I coughed and hacked up mucus from this lingering cold and spat it in his face, daring him to do anything about it. Jay looked at me, wiped his face and rubbed my mucus on Nika's arm. "Fucking bastard," I thought.

"Are they discharging you today," Jay asked sternly?

"Yes," Nika responded.

"Good, I'll take you home and get you away from these crazy bitches," Jay snarled.

LACE

All sorts of thoughts started running through my head when I saw Jay standing at the door. "Did this idiot leave my friend for dead and think he would just go stand duty? What kind of narcissist was he? Did this motherfucker bathe and got dressed while my friend lay on the cold kitchen floor, clinging to life? I immediately felt the blood rush up into my veins and through my body. I was hot. I lunged toward Jay, but Jen and Sasha stopped me before I reached my target. And that son of a bitch laughed.

SASHA

I couldn't believe it. We were all in disbelief. "Nika, if you go home with this bastard, don't ever fucking call me again!" Lace screamed as she stormed out.

Jen looked at me and back to Nika, grabbed her things, and announced, "I'm with Lace on this one. I can't stand by and watch you get yourself killed. What are you doing, Sasha?" Jen asked.

I walked over to Nika and hugged her as tight as I could and whispered in her ear, "I love you, and I release you." As I let her go, Nika began to cry uncontrollably. I grabbed my things and Jen, and I walked arm and arm out of the door with tears of our own.

I called Lace. She had already made it down to the lobby, where she sat waiting for us. We all walked to the car silently, not mentioning Jay, Nika, or the pain we carried for our friend. Lace climbed in the back seat. Her eyes were swollen as were ours. "Aren't you tired of crying?" Lace asked.

"I've cried more since I've been back than I had in the last 9 months," Lace said.

"Jen and I want to talk to you about something important," I responded softly.

We pulled up to Lace's, and she got out of the car and opened the door to her house. I walked in straight past her to the kitchen. "I'm pouring a drink; do you want one?" I asked aloud. No one responded, so I poured myself a shot and drank it fast—toasting to nothing at all.

Lace walked in, finally taking note of her house, looking over every item that had been delivered, unpacked, and placed purposely. She was in deep thought, and she began to rearrange the large sofa that was positioned on the wall that faced the dining room. "Whose idea was it to put the sofa here?" she asked. "Let me hear your concept, then maybe it can stay," she continued.

"Lace," Jen said firmly, "sit down! Let's talk. It's important."

"Is it?" Lace asked.

"Is it about how you recognized Marcus last night?" she asked firmly.

I looked at Jen as she turned beet red, and I responded, "You're tripping Lace. You've shown us plenty of pictures. How else would we know Marcus? Anywho, we don't have time for your Marcus bullshit right now. We need to discuss something important. Jen and I have a plan to kill Jay. We need you onboard."

"What the fuck, Sasha? We can't keep doing this shit!" Lace yelled. "It's not like we're serial killers or anything. It'll be our second kill. God forgives all!" Jen chimed.

"Third," Lace announced without thinking.

"What do you mean third?" Jen asked.

"I don't know what she's talking about," I responded quickly. "Seriously?" Jen asked as she threw her hands in the air.

"Are you guys serious?" Jen continued.

"Nika, just told us it wasn't Jay. We all know it was, but if she doesn't give a damn, why should we?" Lace asked sincerely.

"Because we're better than that, Lace. She's scared, and you know it. She would do it for us," I gently reminded her.

"I wouldn't be in that situation!" Lace shouted.

"You've been in much worse situations," Jen yelled, "and we've had your fucking back! Don't get righteous now!" Jen continued.

"We've talked about this before, Lace. Hear us out before you decide," I asked calmly. It was finally time to fill Lace in on everything that had happened while she was deployed. We told her everything. Every beating she missed that Nika had been subjected to. We told her about the black eyes, the cracked ribs, and the knots on her head.

Lace still wasn't onboard until we told her about the night Jay forced a loaded gun up Nika's pussy. He thought she was cheating on him. Since she wanted to fuck someone other than Jay, he made her fuck a loaded gun. He shoved it up her pussy and then her ass until she bled. Lace sat silently, getting angrier by the moment at us for not telling her while she was on deployment, but mostly at Jay.

"The beatings are getting worse, Lace. He's going to kill her! And you know as well as I do, the good ole boy Navy network will protect Jay at every cost," I concluded.

CHAPTER 11
LACE

"Snap out of it, Lace, and come on!" Jen motioned. I was in a daze. I couldn't believe the story I just heard. "Who does that? Who sticks loaded guns up his wife's pussy?" I followed Sasha and Jen through the kitchen and into the garage. I couldn't understand why my friend would stay in an abusive and demeaning marriage. I couldn't wrap my thoughts around it.

The garage was empty, dark, and cold. I assumed there would be a few boxes left me to go through in the garage, but there was nothing. They literally unpacked everything for me. "Why are we back here?" Neither Jen nor Sasha said a word. Jen turned to the left and hit the switch on the right to turn on the light. Sasha reached to the right and grabbed the attic pole. She swung it above her head and latched it onto the attic hook on the first try. The attic door opened, and Sasha pulled the stairs down. She pulled them all the way out and locked them in place. I did not even know I had an attic, let alone attic stairs. Sasha went up first. Then Jen, then me. Once I reached the top of the attic, I lifted myself up to get all the way in. I dusted off my knees and stood up. I thought it was kind of funny that the three of us could stand straight up in an attic.
"What are you smiling about? Jen asked.
I looked up, and as I opened my mouth to say "nothing," I saw exactly why we were in the attic.

Sasha and Jen looked at me and didn't say anything. I stood there, pondering the situation in complete silence. Paying close attention to the attic as it was completely covered with clear plastic and blue traps draped over it. The ceiling, walls, window, everything was covered. Everything except an empty metal folding chair. Jen finally broke the silence by simply asking, "Are you in, Lace?" I stayed silent.

Sasha led us back downstairs. As she passed through the kitchen, she grabbed a bottle of vodka and three cups that must have been placed there purposefully. We headed to my bedroom. Jen secured the attic door with a stick and a lock. I had only been in my house a handful of times. Once for the first look, then inspection, appraisal, the final walk-through, and last night when I cried myself to sleep. It was hard to believe it was really my house. It didn't quite feel like home, though. There wasn't a lick of dust anywhere. Nika hired Keys to Klean LLC, a housekeeping company, to keep the house clean and free of dust while I was deployed. I made a mental note to thank her and pay her back what she had spent.

Sasha led us back to my bedroom and sat on the bed. She got really comfortable. She placed the bottle of vodka on the nightstand next to her. Jen followed Sasha's lead as I checked out my closets. I checked out my bathroom this morning before we left as I showered. It felt good to take a shower in my own bathroom without being bothered by another impatiently waiting female sailor, standing way too close to me, waiting on a free shower. Boat life was for the birds, and I was glad to be off the ship.

I joined the girls on the bed. I sat Indian style with my back toward the door while Sasha and Jen sat with their backs against the headboard. Sasha poured us each a cup of straight vodka. We sipped slowly and talked about accomplishing our immediate goal. Clearly, this idea was not fresh to Sasha. She had everything planned—from how we would kill Jay, get rid of the body, and our alibies.

"Let me get this straight, Sasha. You want to kidnap Jay, torture him, peel the skin off his body and slice his throat in my attic, then do a science project in my bathtub of lye and sulfuric acid and hope for the best?" I asked through uncontrollable laughter. I couldn't control myself. I literally could not stop laughing. "That's the dumbest shit I ever heard, Sasha! It's so over the top," I said. "Who's torturing and peeling his skin? Who's cutting his throat? Sasha, you have been watching too many murder shows. That shit is unrealistic. We're not that evil, I hope," I concluded.
"What's your plan? We've done worse!" Sasha shot back. I shot Sasha a shut the fuck up glance.
"I didn't even know I needed a plan until a few minutes ago. I didn't know my friend was being sodomized by fucking loaded guns, Sasha," I yelled. "The fuck give me a goddam minute to process this shit!" I screamed.

I was so angry, but I was sure I could come up with something better than torturing someone in the attic." After a few minutes of thinking, I said, "Let's just shoot him and dump his body in the lake behind the house.
"You want to dump his body in the lake behind your house?" Sasha asked.
"Yes, I do. I'm sure there is plenty of dead bodies back there. This Saturday would be perfect," I said with excitement.
"Why Saturday?" Jen asked.
"We'll all have alibis. My welcome home party is Saturday, and everyone will be here. If the cops ever suspected this location or us, they wouldn't find anything because the area would be contaminated. They

wouldn't be able to obtain any real evidence. We can include a bonfire in the evening events and burn the clothes we will wear to kill him afterward. It's perfect," I said as I jumped off the bed. I started pacing. It's what I do when I have a great idea, or when I'm angry as hell. I was both at the moment. I continued, "This way, no one else is involved. I'm taking it you had help getting all that stuff in the attic, right? Sasha?"

"Tony helped," Sasha replied.

"We don't need outsiders in our business. Let's keep this between us," I insisted.

JEN

"Lace's idea is good. I like it, but we would have to tweak it some. Where would you get a gun from? If we use one of ours, it will be too obvious. We can't buy one because it will be a paper trail, and we wouldn't get it in time," I asked as Lace continued pacing.

Lace then turned to me, smiled, and said, "We'll use Jay's gun. We'll kill that fucking asshole with his own piece! We'll toss it in the lake when we're done."

"Lace, you are out of your mind," Sasha noted. "How the hell do you plan on getting Jay's gun?" Sasha asked with concern.

Without even thinking, I responded, "From Nika. We all just walked out on one of our best friends over Jay. I know she must want him gone too."

"I don't know, Jen, she really loves him," Sasha announced.

"Does she really?" Sasha. Lace just saw her all hugged up with some random. I've been picking DD up a lot lately due to her 'working late" but not wanting Jay to know. What if all this time she was spending time with Lamar?" I asked.

"They did look rather cozy," Lace co-signed.

"We'll have to bring Nika in on this if we want to use Jay's gun. If Jay had duty yesterday, his next duty day would be Thursday or Friday. We can get the gun then. We need to figure out which one and see if Nika is onboard," I continued.

"I think it's best if Nika doesn't know. She's too weak and may flip," Sasha replied.

"How do you suggest we get his gun then, Sasha? Nika has to be in," I insisted. "Lace, what say you?"

Lace continued pacing. After about two minutes, she finally responded, "Nika hasn't flipped yet, and we've done some shit. I don't think she loves Jay like we think she does. I'm with Jen, Sasha. We need Nika for this."

We started making and changing plans. Giving suggestions and ideas and creating new ones. We talked about everything, the important details and the minute ones. We talked so much that we didn't keep track of the time. Robbie and Carter expected us to stay out over the weekend, but it was nearing time for me and Sasha to make it home and prepare ourselves and the kids for the week. Lace was still on leave and had all the time in the world.

"OK! I think we have it all together," I finally announced. We all agreed on the final plan. Everyone knew their roles and timelines.

"It's time for me to get home. Robbie has had Alisha all weekend. I know he's about ready to lose it," I announced.

"I need to head home, too," Sasha added. "I'm sure Carter is out of his mind, especially after Friday night," Sasha continued as she laughed hysterically. Lace and I followed suit, laughing at Sasha's Friday night shenanigans. I hugged and kissed both Sasha and Lace as we always did when we parted ways. Sasha and I walked to our cars still laughing about Friday night.

The drive home was long and draining. I was so over Jay, thinking he could treat my friend like shit. I would have killed him by myself if Sasha and Lace weren't onboard. We had all lost someone, and all managed to get over the heartbreak. "Nika will get over this one just fine. Axel passed, and I'm over it. Mostly over it. Well, most days, I'm completely healed."

Lace and Sasha's comments and eye-rolls had me thinking about Axel.

#####

Robbie and I were never the same after I caught him fucking Petty Officer McKnight. It was easy for Axel to slide in. I met Axel while I was in nursing school, doing an internship at a nursing home in Greenbriar. I was working the night shift. I was just starting and barely finding my way.

A team of contractors was brought up from North Carolina to build an addition to the nursing home. They did most of their work at night too. Axel was one of the contractors. He was gorgeous. He looked nothing like Robbie. He was tall buff and brown skin. His skin was smooth as butter. He was an older guy. A little rough around the edges.

Axel and I would flirt with each other in passing. Occasionally, we would add crude conversation to our friendly flirting. Axel was bold. I didn't know just how bold, until one night, I was warming up my lunch, and we bumped into each other in the break room. Axel gave me a devilish smile and asked, "What are you heating up?"

"Salmon and veggies," I said nonchalantly.

"I would love to taste it," Axel responded with his smile now turned seductive. I returned the smile, recognizing he wasn't referring to the food.

"I doubt you could handle it," I said as I walked away.

Later that night, Axel cornered me into an empty room and pinned me up against the wall. He looked at me and smiled and waited patiently for me to silently agree for him to continue. I did. He moved me toward an empty chair. Axel sat me down and yanked my scrubs off. He pulled so hard that I almost slid out of the chair. He buried his face in my pussy as if it belonged to him. I immediately creamed all over him. He refused to let me up. He kept a tight hold on my legs, devouring my pussy, forcing me to cream repeatedly until I literally begged him to stop. When he finally came up, he simply stated, "I guess I can handle it!"

We became secret lovers after that night. Well, it was a secret until Robbie left on his next deployment. Then Axel and I began to see each other openly. We went on dates around town, and instead of going back to North Carolina on the weekends, Axel stayed with Alisha and me.

Axel engaged in recreational drugs, often. I participated in it a time or two. Well, more than I should have for sure. Lace, Sasha and Nika didn't like Axel for that reason alone. They especially hated it when he did drugs around Alisha. I didn't mind so much. She was young and really didn't know what was going on. They often tried to get me to stop seeing Axel, but I was having fun and was in total control of the situation. I was falling for him, too.

I loved spending time with Axel on the weekends, but I thought my friends were a little jealous. They thought I was spending too much time with him. After about four months of Axel and me dating, the girls planned a mommy's play date. It was earlier this year during MLK weekend at Sasha's house. Lace drove down from Maryland to hang out too. Lace and Sasha disappeared shortly after Lace's arrival to run some errands. Nika and I stayed with the kids while they played.

"Did you guys finish up your errands," I asked when they returned.

"We sure did," Lace responded nonchalantly as she high-fived Nika. I didn't think much of it. Lace always said VA had stuff that Maryland didn't have. She had certain stores down here she loved that hadn't made their way to Maryland yet. After she got over her Marcus funk, she would often come down just to go shopping.

I didn't think my friends had anything to do with Axel's death, considering it was an overdose, but Sasha's comments sure had me thinking now, and I always wondered how Sasha and Nika arrived so quickly that night.

"Did they kill Axel that day? If not Axel, then who and why don't I know about it?"

CHAPTER 12
LACE

"I'm starving. I should have had one of them take me to the grocery store before they left. Dammit!" Bald Guy was calling again. It was his third call. My plan was to mail him his funky ass clothes and never speak to him again. I hadn't even planned to wash them first. I was going to ball them up and put them in the mail. I knew he didn't give a damn about the clothes. He just wanted what was in them.

Being carless and hungry was giving me second thoughts, though, about answering Bald Guy's calls. I wasn't scheduled to fly to Miami and pick up T and my truck from Simba until next Sunday after my welcome back party. "What the hell?" I thought. I texted Bald Guy to see if he wanted to see me and of course, he did. I had to give him my address since I had no way to meet him. Not ideal, but I guess this one time wouldn't hurt.

I jumped in the shower to wash the hospital smell off me. I slathered myself with lotion and oils and dressed in a long-sleeve, ankle-length black midi dress. Nothing special as this wasn't a date. Bald Guy showed up as soon as I finished dressing. He pulled up in the driveway as if his car belonged there. I rolled my eyes as I glanced through the blinds. I was still debating on wearing tights when I heard the doorbell ring. He lived by Norfolk International. "He must have run every red light to get here so quickly," I thought. He rang the bell again, but I waited. Pacing, thinking, "Should I really let him in? He's a fucking random for Christ's sake."

He rang the bell again, and I answered, unsure of my next move. "Hey, gorgeous," he said as I moved to the side to let him in.

"Hey, Bald Guy," I responded. "Jaxton! My name is Jaxton," he replied. I laughed so hard… "Who the fuck cares?" was what I wanted to scream, but I decided on something a little sweeter.

"I like Bald Guy better, so I think I'll stick with that." He smiled. His smile was gorgeous; surely, I didn't remember that.

"You mind telling me your name since this is clearly no longer a one-night stand?" he asked.

I smiled and answered truthfully. Although I wanted to give him my alter ego's name, which only came out anytime I was drunk. "My name is Lacey. My friends call me Lace."

"Ah, so we're friends now," Bald Guy responded.

"You can call me Lacey," I shot back quickly.

Bald Guy laughed as he stood uncomfortably close to me and spoke sternly, "You said you were hungry. Let's go grab something to eat!" Since I was starving, I agreed.

I honestly couldn't remember the last time I had eaten. I also didn't remember how handsome this guy was. "My God! Do all my randoms look this good?" I wondered.

"We'll go to Lillian's. It's a seafood restaurant up the street. You like seafood, right?" he asked.

"I sure do," I responded. Bald Guy made the decision on where we would eat without even asking me. I kind of liked that. I was turned on. I slipped on a pair of high calf boots and grabbed my coat out of the closet. We walked out to Bald Guy's car, and he opened the car door for me. I smiled as I thought, "He's laying it on thick!" He walked to the driver's side, got in and put on his seat belt and motioned for me to do the same. As he drove, I couldn't help but notice his bulging package. The restaurant was only about 15 minutes away. I wondered if I had time for a pre-meal appetizer.

I reached over and put my hand in between his legs to make sure my eyes weren't playing tricks on me. They weren't. His dick was rock hard. My pussy got wet. Super wet at the thought of his dick in me. I unzipped his pants and pulled his dick out of his zipper. He jerked, he was a little shy. It was kind of cute. He moved his hand toward his pants to stop me.

I popped his hand. "Stop it! Let him out!" I said. He looked at me nervously and let out a laugh. I took my seat belt off, leaned over and put my head between his legs and wrapped my lips around his shaft while he drove. I began sucking his dick with a purpose. I wrapped my hand around it and stroked up, down and around with my spit again and again while sucking and slurping. I sucked hard and long, while he moaned and drove, carefully, I hoped.

The car finally stopped moving, and I felt his chair move backward. I thought we were parked, but I was not sure, and I wasn't about to stop to find out. I continued sucking and gliding my tongue against his shaft, enjoying every moment of it until he exploded in my mouth. Bald Guy couldn't contain himself; I felt his leg jerking, so I swallowed and started back sucking, horribly mean, I knew. Bald Guy was finally able to pull my mouth away from his dick right as he was about to come again, or so I thought.

"Get out! Get out of the car!" he yelled. I was so confused.
"What?" I asked.
Bald Guy jumped out of the car and rushed to the passenger side.

He yanked me out of the car so fast I didn't have a chance to react. He pushed me up against the car and stood behind me. He hiked my dress up and pulled my panties to the side and, without warning, went straight in. My feet were completely off the ground, and he was fucking me crazily.

I was dazed for a few seconds or minutes, not sure which. When I came through, back to reality, I noticed we were in the parking lot of Lillian's, in clear view of the main road. "He could have at least parked in the back," I thought, but then the thought of strangers watching us turned me on even more. I began to moan louder, begging him to go deeper and harder. Bald Guy had one hand literally holding me up while fingering my pussy and the other fondling my tits. He began playing with my clit while fucking me hard from the back. It was exhilarating. I got weak. My body started to shake, and my pussy became even more slippery as I came. I came hard. My head went backward, and my body shook from pleasure.

Bald Guy finally let me down after I finished convulsing in his arms. "You good?" he asked.

I smiled and responded, "Never better."

I fixed myself, and he did the same. We walked into Lillian's as if nothing had happened.

I leaned over and whispered with a smile, "Are you going to wash your hands?"

He smiled back, "Absolutely not," he responded. We both laughed as we were escorted to our table.

I ordered the seafood linguine and a bottle of Argentinian Malbec. I always ordered the bottle when I went out to eat, regardless of who was paying. If I went on a date and ordered a bottle, and the guy had something to say about it, I knew right then we would never be together. I would tell the waitress to split the check. Ensuring that whomever I was on a date with knew never to call me again. Didn't want a judger thinking I owed him shit for my meal or my bottle.

Bald Guy ordered the land and sea meal and added on scallops. I didn't even have to ask him to order anything different; he just knew dating protocol. He ordered his steak medium, a perfect choice and the way I liked it. Had he ordered it well or well done, I probably would have walked out of the restaurant and hitched hike back home. A well-done steak is a waste of good beef, and I won't waste my time or energy with a man that doesn't know the difference.

Our food arrived quickly, Bald Guy grabbed my hand and prayed over our meals and thanked God for me returning his call. I laughed so hard that I shed a tear. It was hilarious. He giggled, which also but made it clear that he meant what he said. Before taking the first bite of his steak, he asked if I wanted to taste anything on his plate.

My eyes widened. I am super impressed by this random, like fuck yeah. I want to taste all of it. "Who is this guy?" I thought. "He's getting it very right tonight." As we ate, Bald Guy talked a lot, answering every question I had and asked a lot of questions about me. I tried ignoring most of them, but he was rather persistent and kept flashing that damn smile. I didn't share nearly as much as he did, because I was not interested in getting to know him that well. "He's around for a reason!" And that was it. The quicker he realized that, the better off we would both be.

While he talked, I did find out that he was a handyman and liked to fix things. That was perfect. Part of the plan for killing Jay required me to find an unknowing participant to hook up a garage door opener for my garage. I had no intention of ever using or parking in the garage, but we needed it if our plan was going to work.

When we finished our meal, Bald Guy paid the check without even batting his eyes. He flashed me his gorgeous smile again and winked as he handed the waitress his card. Not sure if it was debit or credit, but he wouldn't be around for the long haul, so I guessed it didn't matter. My father always told me if a man must put dinner on a credit card, then he is not the man you want to be with. I didn't totally agree with that concept now that reward points have become such a big hit, but I still remembered it.

Bald Guy tipped according to the suggested 20 percent on the check, but with cash. That made me smile. Jen used to be a waitress, and she always talked about how, when customers leave a tip on their cards, the staff doesn't get it until their paycheck. Yet they were required to pay out the busboys, hostess, and bartenders each night. I wondered if he used to wait tables or worked in a restaurant. I wanted to ask, but I didn't care enough.

We left the restaurant, and on cue, Bald Guy opened the passenger side of the car for me to enter as he had when he picked me up. I was full and no longer horny and ready for the night to end. I was done with him for the evening. When we arrived at my house, I leaned over, kissed him and thanked him for dinner. I also gave him a separate thank you for his services in the parking lot.

I jumped out of the car and closed the door behind me, not waiting for him to respond to anything I had said. He laughed as he too got out of the car and walked to the door. "What the fuck… he doesn't get it?" I stood at my door as he stood there, waiting for me to open it and let him in. I took a deep breath and tried not to roll my eyes as hard as I wanted to, but he didn't care. "Open the door Lacey," he said sternly. Now the eye-roll. "Who does this jerk think he is?" He smiled, "Cute! You still roll your eyes. Really cute,' he said. I couldn't help but laugh when he said that, and I let his ass in.

Seconds after crossing the threshold of the doorway, he threw me on the couch and got on his knees. He ripped my panties off and French-kissed my pussy like it was his fucking job. He put my clit in his mouth and sucked slow and steady until I was about to come, and then he stopped. "What the fuck?" I yelled.

"Shut up!" Bald Guy responded. I didn't know why, but his tone made me smile. Bald Guy stripped naked and lay on the other end of the sofa and motioned for me to sit on his face. I indulged, "Who am I not to feed a man desiring my warm cookies for dessert?"

I woke up thanking God I was still on leave. Drinking an entire bottle of Malbec does something to you. Bald Guy and I fucked all night long. Like it was a fucking marathon or something, and I was exhausted. Pretty sure I was also still drunk. No way sober me would allow this random to stay over. I knew he had to go to work the next day. I remembered him mentioning something about being an officer in the Navy and having to be in for some meetings that day. I wasn't paying close enough attention to get the details right. I did make sure he knew I was only an E- 5 though. It was his responsibility as the senior person to ensure he was not fraternizing with enlisted personnel, not mine.

Nika was heading over today so I could discuss the plan with her. I needed his ass out of here. Jen told her to be here by 8 a.m. since she was on convalescent leave. "Bald Guy, are you going to work today?" I whispered.

Bald Guy rolled over, smiling, "I sure am," he said. His smile was so intoxicating. "How about breakfast before I go?" he asked through his smile. I shot him a get-the-fuck-out glance and responded as nice as I could at that moment.

"I don't have any groceries. I haven't been to the store since I got back from deployment." Bald Guy rolled partially out of bed and grabbed his pants. He opened his wallet and gave me the cash he had and his car keys.

"Portsmouth Commissary is up the street, go grab us some breakfast while I shower and get dressed," he insisted. "Is this guy crazy?" I thought.

"Dude, you don't have any clothes here, and I don't feel like doing all that," I whined.

"I have a bag and my uniform in the car. I'll walk you out and grab it. Come on, hurry up! I can't be too late," he said with an electrifying smile.

He was so fucking enticing, and so, I did as I was instructed.

The commissary didn't open until 9. I guess Mr. Smarty pants didn't know that. I headed to Food Lion, instead. I arrived back from the store and saw no sign of Bald Guy. I heard a hideous sound coming from my bedroom. When I opened the door, I realized it was Bald Guy singing in the shower. I laughed as I heard him singing. It was horrible. Almost as bad as my singing. I looked on the bed and saw his uniform neatly pressed and spread out. "He has literally made himself at home," I thought.

I walked back to the front of the house and prepared a traditional southern breakfast with flare. I guess I was in the mood for cooking after all. I hadn't cooked since before my deployment, but some skills just didn't fade. We enjoyed fried fish and grits with a few pieces of raisin bread, French toast, bacon and eggs while we talked over breakfast.

Bald Guy ate while dressed in nothing but his boxer briefs, T-shirt, and socks. It was quite distracting. I wanted to straddle him. I couldn't keep my mind off fucking him, but I had to stay focused. I needed him to be on his way soon so Nika could come over. We finished our meal, and Bald Guy headed back to the bedroom to finish dressing. I cleared the table and started cleaning the kitchen. I stood at the sink doing the dishes, staring out the window, and playing our plan out in my head. Bald Guy interrupted my thought by standing behind me pressing his dick against my ass and breathing down my neck. I pushed my ass out and pushed him away from me, smiling as I turned around. I couldn't stop smiling. He looked scrumptious in his uniform.

Bald Guy was well put together and smelled so good. I was almost tempted to call him Jaxton. I had to remind myself that he was a random, and randoms don't have names. Bald Guy walked back up to me and kissed me passionately on my lips. He picked me up and walked toward the door. He opened the door, still holding and kissing me. I wanted to stay in that moment.

Bald Guy put me down and walked out. "I'll be back later to pick up my things," Bald Guy yelled.

"What fucking things, you can't leave shit here," I screamed as his sexy ass walked toward his car.

"I'm coming back to put in your garage door opener, remember!" he said as he waved me off.

"Nika, I need a little more time this morning," Lace said from the other end of the phone.

"Can't you just tell me what it is over the phone," I asked.

"No. Didn't Jen already tell you we need to talk in person? I'll call you when I'm ready for you to come. I have a random at the house demanding breakfast," Lace said in a bothersome tone.

I laughed, "And you're cooking it?" I asked.

"Whatever, I'll call you when he leaves," Lace responded.

"Lace, I only have a short window before Jay gets back home, and I don't want to upset him," I said.

"Why, Nika? What's he going to do, beat you and leave you for dead?" Lace responded in the most disdainful tone she could muster.

"Fuck you, Lace!" I yelled as I hung up the phone.

That was low, even for Lacey! Lace always made vicious comments and thought they were acceptable. I fucking hated her some days. In true Lace fashion, she was only concerned about Lace, not me or my wellbeing. "Whatever it is they need to tell me; Jen and Sasha will have to do it. Fuck Lace." I picked up the phone and called Sasha, and she called Jen on three-way.

"I'm over fucking Lace! This bitch is in the middle of a booty call, yet, it's something important you guys want to share with me. Really, is she the only one that can do it?" I asked.

"She's the only one that's off Nika, and we can't discuss it over the phone. By the time either of us gets off, Jay will already be home," Jen responded.

"Nika, you really need to talk to Lace," Sasha demanded. "She loves you for real. She would never do anything to intentionally hurt you," Sasha asserted.

"Are you serious, Sasha? Lace knew all about Jay. She knew he was fucking crazy; that's why she so freely passed him along. Yet she wants to act like she has no idea he is a woman beater. I don't give a fuck about what any of you say. No real friend of mine would have set me up with him," I yelled through the phone.

"You don't mean that, Nika. If you do, did, you wouldn't still be friends with Lace," Jen stated.

"I'm still friends with her because you two won't let the relationship dissolve," I reminded them.

"Nika, you're angry at Lace for something she had no knowledge or control of. You both met him the same day, how could she have possibly known?" Sasha remarked.

"She fucking knew!" I bellowed.

Although I had no proof, I felt it in my spirit. Lace would have never willingly pass on a new sexy random. "I don't care if she was fucking his dad. She had a feeling and passed him along. I believe she fucking knew and that's all that matters." "You're going to have to let that go and get over it. And let's be for real, Nika. Lace hooked you up for a fuck, and you married him on your own," Jen recapped calmly. Those final words which Jen spoke stung deeply. "I'm so fucking mad at Jay and at Lace. Everyone wants me to leave Jay and forgive Lace. Fuck them both!"

That was exactly why I convinced Sasha and Jen to keep quiet about Marcus! She fucked me over with Jay, and I would be damned if I was going to allow her any fucking happiness. Jen and Sasha were ready to tell Lace the moment Marcus came back. I lied to them a lot about Marcus. I told them he tried to sleep with me and how Lace had shared some things with me about him that weren't flattering. Those lies helped influence their decision heavily, and we all remained silent about Marcus' whereabouts and his attempts to contact Lace.

Honestly, I only did it because of the pain she was in. Anything that would have brought her happiness I kept from her. I wanted her to suffer the way I was suffering. "I'm going to fucking tell her today too. Once Lace's fury takes over, she won't speak to any of us, and she will be out of our lives for good!

"Hey," I responded as I answered Lace's call. "It's 11:00 a.m. So much for calling me, right?" "She doesn't care about anyone except her fucking self," I thought silently.

"Nika, are you on your way?" Lace spoke, interrupting my thoughts.

"Yes," I responded almost in a whisper. A part of me was scared to go to Lace's alone, especially if I planned on telling her about Marcus. I drove to Lace's, thinking about how the three of them walked out on me yesterday, and now they wanted to talk about something important. "I don't know if any of these bitches can be trusted. We've done so much shady shit in the name of "protecting our friends." It's quite ridiculous. One of us is always left in the dark. How can you trust friends like that? My trust in them has been shaky since, Axel."

Although I agreed with it at the time, Jen and Axel didn't deserve what we did to them. Jen loved him, but he had some problems, and Jen was starting to go down the rocky path with him. We couldn't allow that to happen. We had to think about Alisha. We didn't want her growing up with a drug addict as a mother or growing up without a mother at all.

Jen still didn't know that we had anything to do with Axel's overdose. Axel was a good guy, he just had some problems, which Jen couldn't afford. I felt bad for Jen. We held her and cried with her the night she found Axel dead. We showed up as if it was news to us.

It was cruel, but also necessary to get Axel out of the picture. I would think about it and get sick to my stomach. I tried talking to Sasha and Lace about how I felt, but cold-hearted Lace would say, "Well, if he wasn't an addict, it wouldn't have been so easy. We didn't force him to take the drugs. He took them on his own. He killed himself," and then Lace would laugh. We were surely going to hell on a one-way ticket for all the shit we had done.

The only person I completely trusted now was Lamar, and our friendship had gotten shaky too. I hadn't spoken to him since he left the hospital. I tried calling, but he didn't answer. I texted a few times too, and still no response.

I pulled into Lace's driveway as her front door swung open. Lace rushed out and met me at the car. She hugged me. Her embrace was warm and loving. I knew Lace meant well, but sometimes she was just so fucking evil and heartless. She wasn't always like that. Something in her changed after that incident with Sargent Hendricks. She was never the same after that. Lace kissed my cheek and helped me into the house. I could walk fine, but she insisted on helping. "You need anything? Want a glass of wine?" Lace asked.

"No! Just tell me what's going on and why I needed to come over here," I responded sternly.

"Well, Nika," Lace started speaking. "Remember when Jen was pregnant with Axel's baby, and we all agreed that neither Axel nor the baby was good for Jen?" Lace asked. I didn't respond. Lace knew damn well that I remembered. I just stared at her until she continued.

"After Axel died, Jen got her life back on track. She had an abortion, went to that outpatient drug program, and finished nursing school. She hasn't touched any type of drugs since."

"What's your point, Lace?" I asked.

"Sometimes, we must remove the bad parts of ourselves to become who we are supposed to be. Jay is the bad part of you, and he needs to be removed," Lace continued.

"Is this what you'll wanted? I know I need to leave Jay. I know I need to divorce him. You didn't have to call me over here for this shit," I responded.

"Nika, we have a better plan. A plan where Jay meets Sargent Hendricks and Axel. You and DD make out much better than a divorce this way," Lace revealed.

"Why would I agree to kill my husband? You sound ridiculous," I asked in disbelief.

"Because he's a fucking woman beater and a rapist, and we kill rapists. Or have you forgotten?"

CHAPTER 13
JEN

Lace's neighbor had two young boys who had begged for a dog last Christmas. Their parents got them a Labrador retriever. Lace met the dog during her inspection. He was friendly and playful. His coat was silky black. He was gorgeous for a dog. The boys would play outside with the dog for hours in their backyard. When it was time for the dog to poop, they would take the dog on a stroll around the neighborhood. They would allow the dog to poop on the neighbors' lawn and sidewalk and never clean up his shit. I think the boys were much too young for that type of responsibility.

It made Lace's other neighbors furious. They would often complain to us while we were setting up Lace's household goods. We gave Lace a heads-up about the dog and told her that we often found dog shit in her yard. Lace would simply reply, "I'll deal with that shit when I return." Today, Lace was thankful for the dog's shit.

On our way to Nika's, she grabbed an old rag that had been left in the garage by the previous owners. She opened the dried-up rag and filled it with the lab's fresh dog shit. Lace and I drove silently over to Nika's apartment. Sasha followed behind. When we arrived, Lace, Sasha, and I crept slowly into Nika's apartment, using the spare key she dropped off by Lace's earlier in the week. We crept up the stairs into Nika and Jay's bedroom. Jay lay there, sleeping so peacefully. Lace shoved her gun into his face. "Get the fuck up," she yelled. Jay awoke, startled, his eyes wide. He looked to his side and saw Nika sitting there, looking scared.

The one-time Nika had no reason to fear him, but she was still scared. Jay slowly got out of bed. He wore nothing. He was blessed. I saw why Nika fell for his ass.

"Nika, give him something to put on," I demanded. Nika got out of the bed and started fumbling through some drawers.

"What the fuck are you doing? Didn't you know this was happening today? Why don't you have this shit ready?" I asked.

Jay started laughing and said, "You scary bitches aren't going to do shit. That dumb bitch can't even grab clothes," he said, referring to Nika. As soon as the word clothes left Jay's mouth, Lace, using all the strength she could muster up, hit him over the head with her gun. Jay hit the floor in agony. "Stupid bitch," he yelled!

"Chill out, Lace! Let's stick to the plan," Sasha whispered.

Nika finally tossed some pajamas on the floor where Jay had fallen. "Put them on," I instructed. Jay did as he was told without hesitation.

"Where's Jay's gun?" Sasha asked.

Nika walked around the bed while Jay was still dressing and pointed to a side table in the corner of their bedroom. I grabbed Jay's gun. Sasha zip-tied Jay's hands behind his back, and we got him on his feet. I walked in front, and Lace walked behind Jay with her gun to his back and ushered him down the stairs. We coaxed Jay into my car. Jay was talking, trying his best to fight us. Lace must have expected that. She shoved the dirty rag filled with dog shit into Jay's mouth. It was disgusting. I almost threw up as I watched through the rear-view mirror. I started the car and headed straight for Lace's.

It was a straight shot to Lace's house from Nika's. I took the military highway and hit a right onto George Washington. We got to Lace's in no time. Lace's new random hooked up the garage door opener Monday, and it was working like a charm. I pulled into the garage and parked. Lace and I got out of the car. Lace still had her gun pointed directly at Jay's head, but he refused to move. Jay fought us the entire time, making me angrier and angrier. I hated Jay. I hated him for everything he'd done to my friend. A part of me wished we would have had Tony and his friends kidnap Jay and bring him to us. Jay was strong and wasn't going down without a fight. We had all agreed to no-blood-in-the-car or the house, but he wouldn't stop fucking fighting and kicking at us.

There was only one way to cripple him, I thought. I picked up Jay's gun and mustered up every bit of strength I had. I waited for one of his kicks toward Lace and hit him right in his balls with his gun handle. Jay buckled over in the backseat. Lace looked at me, smiled, and hi-fived me. "Perfect!" she said. We yanked his black ass out of the car and dropped him on the cold garage ground. Jay had been calling us crazy for years. Now he was about to see firsthand just how crazy we were.

While Jay lay on the garage floor, refusing to move, I secured the dog shit-filled rag in his mouth with duct tape. I wrapped the tape completely around Jay's head, covering his nose mouth and ears. I placed the unused tape in a garbage bag. There were three separate bags. All the things we used would be put in separate bags for easy disposal.

"Why the fuck do we keep doing this dumb shit?" I asked myself. Still, every time, I agreed. I was not cut from the same cloth. I was so engaged in my thoughts. I was running out of the house behind Sasha and almost forgot Jay's phone. Sasha was in her car, waiting impatiently, but not bringing any attention to herself. She followed me as I drove Jay's car. It was déjà vu all over again, except this time it was in Norfolk instead of Severn.

We headed toward the Norfolk Naval base. I drove carefully, not to be noticed. Once on base, I parked near Jay's command and waited for Sasha to arrive. I thought she was right behind me, but I guess we got separated somehow. I dropped Jay's phone down the side of the seat as I was instructed to do. They literally thought everything out. I guess it was easier this time around, considering the mistakes we made the first time. I couldn't help but think about why I agreed to do this. "Was it a selfish decision, or was it the right decision? What effect would this have on DD?" I wondered. I figured it couldn't be any worse than her burying her mother. Jay didn't love me; I was convinced. There was no way someone could love you and beat you as he beat me. I was scared but relieved at the same time.

Sasha pulled up next to me just as planned. I got out of Jay's car and got into Sasha's. Sasha looked at me and smiled. "It's over now, Nika." I smiled, but I was worried. I knew she hadn't spoken to Lace or Jen, because her phone was with them. My phone was at my house, and there was no way for us to call them. She had no idea if it was really over. We just had to hope everything went according to the plan.

"We're murders. Not just regular murders, we're serial killers, Sasha," I whispered softly.

"Girl, please. Fuck them, niggas! We're making the world a better place. Nobody's going to miss a rapist, drug addict, and a womanizer! If they do, then they're fools," Sasha replied.

"DD will miss Jay," I whispered. We rode back to my house in silence.

Sasha hugged me tight as we walked up to my door. "I'll see you in a bit, Nika. Don't be late," Sasha continued. I smiled.

"I'm going to shower. Then I'll head to my mom's to grab DD and be on my way. I should arrive right behind you," I informed her. Sasha raised her hand for our parting high five. We would often high-five once we accomplished something great. High fives weren't just reserved for murders. They were for all accomplishments: promotions, weddings, babies, and everything. It just seemed like lately, we were high-fiving murders more than anything else. Well, I guess that was not totally true. Jen did finish nursing school recently, and Lace brought her second house. We high-fived those accomplishments too. I guess the murder high fives just weighed heavier on me.

I opened my door and walked up the stairs to my apartment. A sense of peace rushed over my body. I felt an overwhelming sense to cry. I walked to the bathroom, got undressed, and glanced at my bruised body in the mirror. "No more bruises. No more broken bones. No more black eyes," I whispered to myself. "No more pains," I shouted as my eyes swelled with tears. I turned on the shower and got in, and I cried. Tears of joy, I thought or maybe relief. I wasn't sure which one it was. I stood there for a long while, not bathing, just crying.

I finally bathed, and as I turned off the shower, I heard banging on my door. It was just after 8: 00 a.m. "Who the hell could it be?" I thought. I grabbed my towel and wrapped myself in it. "It must be Sasha," I thought as I ran down the stairs to the door. I looked through the peephole and saw that it was Lamar. I debated opening the door. I was sure he saw my car, though. I missed him. I missed him like crazy. We had never gone an entire week without seeing each other. I was miserable without him. I really wanted to see him, but I wasn't sure if I was mentally ready to face Lamar. But I was longing to be in his presence.

I opened the door slowly. "Hey! I've been worried about you," he spoke softly with a hint of anxiety in his voice. I hid slightly behind the door as I was only wearing a towel. He took note of me wearing nothing but a towel. Lamar pushed the door completely open and hugged me. His embrace was as warm as always. "I've called you several times," Lamar continued.

"My phone's broken," I announced, as I tightened my towel that had become loose. My phone wasn't broke; it was a lie. That was the first lie I ever told Lamar. I saw his calls, but I was too scared to talk to him. I thought I might tell him something that he shouldn't know, so I ignored him just as he ignored me Monday and Tuesday. I was also upset with him, but I would never tell him that. He hadn't even attempted to call me until the previous night. An entire week had gone by almost. We hadn't gone a day without speaking since last year.

I always assumed that if he was not talking or spending time with me, he was spending it with Leni. Although he would never admit that, he would always use his daughter as his reason for everything. He had one daughter and five sons. I didn't know why the thought of him with his wife made me jealous. He must have known because he never mentioned her by name. I mean, she was his wife. There was some expectation of intimacy, I guessed. Still, I hated the thought of her having his time, any of his time. I wanted all of it. I never thought the kids took up his time. They had each other and their own friends. I always assumed it was her. Regardless of what he told me, I was pretty sure it was.

I never met Leni. I had seen pictures of her. She was beautiful. She and Lamar looked good together. He had pictures of them all over his desk at work. I used to sit and imagine myself in her place. He loved her or maybe the idea of what she represented. I would picture him with her often: sometimes cuddling on the sofa, and having conversations reserved for just the two of them. I would picture him kissing her gently with the lips I wanted solely on me. When my mind really got the best of me, I would picture her ridding his dick and him enjoying it. The thought of her enjoying the dick I wanted in me made me sick, literally sick. I wanted to ride his dick, kiss his lips, and cuddle with him, although I would never admit that to him or anyone else for that matter.

"What are you doing here?" I asked.

Lamar stood there silent, searching my face for what I was not sure of.

"Where is Jay?" Lamar asked.

"He's on duty. He left this morning. Why'd you ask?" I questioned. Lamar just stood there waiting for something more. He clearly did not like my answer.

"You really shouldn't be here. Jay could pop up at any time. You know how Saturday duty can be. You should probably leave before he comes back. I don't want any problems," I continued. The second lie I would tell Lamar.

The lies were rolling out of my lips to the one man I had never lied to. Lamar could sense something was wrong, or I was lying. I went silent. I wasn't sure if I should keep talking or stay silent. Lamar was standing in front of me, just staring me in my eyes. I loved it when he stared at me and I at him. It was our way of communicating with no words.

"Let me in Nika," Lamar demanded. I moved to the side to allow Lamar to enter. As he came in, he grabbed my hand and closed the door. My towel was struggling to stay in place. He walked up the stairs, leading the way for me to follow.

"I only have a few minutes. I need to get to Lace's to help with the party," I announced. A part of me was relieved Lamar, and I hadn't spoken. I would have told him about Lace, Sasha, and Jen walking out on me at the hospital. Then I would have had to explain why I was still going to Lace's party, which would have led to me explaining our plan for Jay. In this instance, "The less he knows, the better," I thought.

Lamar ignored my comments, and my towel woes and sat on the sofa. I sat beside him. The towel was barely covering my pussy while I was standing. When I sat down, it rode up and exposed my pussy. "Let me go put on some clothes," I insisted as I jumped up off the sofa.

Lamar jumped up too. "May I," Lamar asked as he stood. He reached for my towel and opened it. Removing it from my body and dropped it on the sofa.

Lamar gazed at my broken and bruised body. He turned me around to get a complete look. When I turned back around, his eyes were watery. He handed me back my towel. I didn't take it. I let it fall to the floor. He picked it up and covered my naked body. Once I was covered, Lamar grabbed me and embraced me tightly, whispering soft apologies in my ear. I wanted to tell him it wasn't his fault. But a part of me felt like it was. I loved him, and he loved me, why didn't he protect me?

Reality hit hard as those thoughts raced through my mind. It was not his responsibility. I was not his wife. That was why. I stood there silently in his arms while he continued to mumble useless apologies. My body was so comfortable in his arms. I wanted him to kiss and caress me. But he didn't. He just held me closely, not wanting to let go. When he finally released me, he kissed me softly on the forehead and told me he had to go.

Tears formed in my eyes. I didn't know why. I couldn't stop the tears from falling. I didn't just love Lamar. I was in love with him, and for the first time, I felt completely rejected by him. "Please don't cry, Nika. Please," Lamar asked softly. He didn't ask why I was crying. He just asked me not to. But I couldn't stop. I wanted him to stay with me, to comfort me just a little while longer.

"Why can't you stay?" I asked through my tears.

"I have a thing with the girl," he said. That was his response to everything. The girl was his daughter. He never used his wife as an excuse, although I knew "the girl" was interchangeable for wife and daughter. I never knew for sure if he couldn't, or he wouldn't stay. I just knew he didn't. Lamar left without saying another word.

I didn't walk him out. Instead, through tears and sobs, I asked that he lock the door behind him. I was on an emotional roller coaster; I didn't have time for that shit today. I needed to stay focused! I walked into my bedroom and slathered my body with lotion, with tears still in my eyes. "Stop it, Nika. You look foolish, right? Right!" I told myself.

"I know Lamar, and I will never be. I know he'll never choose me. Why am I crying about something I already know?" I pulled myself together while I considered what I would wear today. I hadn't planned on wearing a bra, so I needed to wear a dark-colored shirt. I reached in the drawer and pulled out a green T-shirt. I slipped it on, and fear crippled me as I heard the door open. "Oh, my God! What if it's Jay?" I thought. I didn't walk out of the room. I was scared. I didn't know what to do. "If that's Jay, where is Sasha, Jen and Lace?"

I heard the footsteps coming down the hallway. I had given Jay's gun to the girls, so I had no way to protect myself from Jay's anger. I just stood there, not breathing or moving, until I saw a comforting shadow in the doorway.

I let out a huge sigh, followed by a rush of tears and comments, "I thought you were Jay. I was so scared. I thought... I thought."

"You thought what, Nika?" Lamar asked.

"Nothing. I thought you were Jay, that's all," I responded in almost a whisper.

"Where is Jay?" Lamar asked again, sternly.

"How did you get in?" I asked sternly. Lamar did not answer me; instead, he waited for a response to his question.

"As I told you earlier, he's on duty," I responded with a hit of nervousness in my voice. Lamar gave me a questionable look. I knew that he knew I was lying. Why else would he be here? Lamar walked into the bedroom and looked around. He sat on the bed and motioned for me to sit down next to him.

He interrupted me from getting dressed. I had only gotten as far as putting on a T-shirt. The shirt wasn't long enough to cover my pussy, and it rose as I sat down. I didn't even try to pull it down to cover myself. I left my pussy exposed for Lamar to see. He tried to ignore it, but it was quite distracting. "Are you going to tell me the truth?" Lamar asked again.

"Well, he is supposed to be on duty, but you're asking as if you know he's not there, so why you don't tell me?" I snapped. I knew I was caught, but what does Lamar know?

Lamar was quiet. He wanted to say something but opted not to reveal whatever he thought he knew. I turned toward him, opening my legs slightly. Lamar looked down and put a hand on each leg and pushed my legs together, closing them. He held them together while he stared at me. I smiled, not saying anything, waiting for him to make a move or leave. This was my first time ever being so bold with Lamar.

We sat there staring at each other, not saying a word for several minutes. Lamar finally leaned over and kissed me. It was a rush. He slipped his tongue in my mouth, and we shared our first kiss. It was long, sensual, and wet. I began to slide forward, as he was still kissing me. I moved his hand from my leg to my breast, and he began to fondle them under my shirt. He then moved his lips from my lips to my bruised and battered breast.

I then guided his hands from my breast to my pussy. He sucked on my breast gently, circling my nipples with his tongue. His fingers found their way inside my exposed pussy. I could feel him slip his middle finger in. I was warm and wet. He began fingering me. I was supposed to be headed to Lace's by now, I thought, but I had waited too long for Lamar, and I wasn't about to stop now.

I moved my hips with the motion of Lamar's fingers in my pussy. He then repositioned himself in between my legs and moved his lips off my breast. He kissed my bruised stomach as he made his way down to my wet pussy. Lamar pushed my legs open and took note of my neatly shaven pussy. He admired it for a few seconds before he began to kiss it slowly.

He kissed every inch of my pussy, placing extra soft, wet, kisses on my clitoris before he buried his face in. He tongue-fucked me until I couldn't take anymore. Then he moved back up to my clit, sucking, nibbling, and circling it until I came.

I shoved Lamar slightly away and demanded he stand up. He did as he was instructed. I pulled his pants down, and his dick popped out at attention.

He was fully erect. I took my time, admiring his dick. "It's thick and long, much bigger than I expected," I said with a smile.

I instructed Lamar to lie down. He opted to lie on the floor. I stood up and removed my shirt. I sat my pussy on his face and leaned forward and began sucking his dick. After only a few sucks and strokes, Lamar climaxed in my mouth and I in his. I climbed off Lamar, pussy still soaking wet. I sat my warm wet pussy on Lamar's softening dick. I rubbed his dick on my pussy until it grew enough to go inside of me. His dick hardened once inside. I rode him slow and steady.

We stared in each other eyes, neither of us saying a word. He guided my hips with his hands until we both came. I lay on top of him as I interlocked our fingers. I kissed Lamar on his lips and whispered in his ear, "It's about damn time." We both laughed hysterically.

We lay there silently for a few more minutes. "It's time for me to leave, babe," Lamar whispered.

I smiled. It was his first time calling me anything other than my name, and I liked it.

CHAPTER 14
SASHA

As I pulled up to Lace's house, the surroundings felt eerie. The energy was different. I walked up to the house, hoping everything was done and went according to the plan. The music was loud. I opened the door, not knowing what to expect. A smile graced my face as I saw Lace and Jen dancing in their underwear and bras. "I take it everything went according to the plan?" I yelled over the music.

Lace turned the music down, just enough for me to hear her reply, "Old happy trigger did her thing." They both laughed. I wasn't sure what that meant exactly, but they were excited about it. I was just glad it was over. We all laughed.

"How did things go with Nika?" Jen asked.

"As planned. She said she was going to shower, grab DD and head this way," I responded.

"What time is Robbie dropping Alisha?" I asked.

"He's dropping her around two," Jen responded.

"Carter is bringing the boys over around the same time," I acknowledged.

"Hey, cut the chatter. Bald Guy just pulled up. Go put on some clothes," Lace demanded.

"You invited him?" I asked with a huge grin on my face.

"Well, he kind of invited himself, and I didn't have the heart to say no," Lace responded.

Jen busted out laughing and asked, "Since when you don't have the heart to say no to anyone?"

Lace ignored Jen as she walked behind her to the bedroom to throw something on. Jen threw on some sweats and a top and was done before Bald Guy could ring the doorbell. Jen headed straight to the kitchen and opened another bottle of wine. We still had plenty of cooking to do, and we couldn't do it without wine! Jen poured three glasses of sweet Walter red as Lace reappeared from the back.

She handed us our glasses and proposed a toast. "To no more Jay," she whispered. We raised our glasses, tapped them, and drank.

"Why are we toasting without Nika?" I asked.

"Because she's not here, and we're about to be in mixed company," Jen responded.

Lace motioned for me to be silent, as she opened the front door. Lace greeted the random like she was happy to see him. Jen and I looked at each other strangely. "Hey, you guys remember Bald Guy? Bald Guy, this is Sasha and Jen," Lace announced.

"It's nice to meet you," I said, staring Lace down.

"Same here," Jen responded. We both couldn't believe how happy Lace was to see this random.

Lace issued the random instructions after instructions. As she was talking, he backed her into the wall and kissed her hard. Jen and I couldn't believe it. Lace didn't even resist him. Instead, she threw her arms around him and joined in.

When Bald Guy was done kissing Lace, he backed up and asked, "Where do you want me to start?"

Lace had the biggest smile on her face. She answered him in a voice we rarely heard. Her voice that was reserved for lovers and friends, but NOT randoms. Lace was hard on randoms. She didn't treat them like real people. She just used them as she saw fit and talked to them any way she wanted, but it was never in a soft sweet voice.

"The tables are in Jen's car, you can start there," Lace responded.

"What in the flying fuck is going on here?" I asked once Bald Guy left the room.

Lace just smiled sheepishly and responded, "Nothing, he's just a random."

"Are you sure? You seem mightily smitten over there," Jen noted.

"Shut up. I just met the damn guy. You two are ridiculous," Lace continued.

"How many times have you seen him since y'all met last week?" I asked. Lace ignored me because she knew if it was more than twice, then that would be the tell-tell sign of him being more than just a random. The next few hours were spent cooking and talking as we danced to random songs. For a split second, I had déjà vu of us dancing in Lace's town-house in Severn to these same songs. It was the weekend Sargent Hendricks disappeared.

Robbie and Carter dropped off the kids. Carter planned on coming back a little later, but I was hoping he didn't because I had already invited Tony. I hadn't seen Tony since last Friday, and I was in need of a fix. Robbie had returned from his deployment a week ago. He was trying desperately to get back into Jen's good graces. He even stayed around for a bit to help Bald Guy, whose name was apparently Jaxton, with some of his delegated chores.

Lace slipped up and called Bald Guy by his name twice, and he loved it. Jen and I could tell because each time she said Jaxton, his dick got hard. It was crazy.

"How much time do you think they have spent together?" Jen whispered to me.

"I'm not sure, I know he took her to buy all the groceries for the party Wednesday, and they had dinner Thursday," I said.

"They had dinner Sunday night and breakfast Monday morning, too," Jen added. "Well, that's four days for sure. She's spent the entire week with a random," Jen declared. We both laughed. This was nothing like Lace. She was feeling this dude.

NIKA

"Where the fuck are you?" Jen yelled into the phone.

"I'm on my way, I'm sorry I got hung up," I responded quickly.

"Why the fuck didn't you call?" Jen asked.

"I couldn't call. I had company, and well, I just couldn't call. I'll be there soon," I said as I hung up. I didn't want Jen asking me any more questions. I needed to come up with a reason I was so late. I arrived at Mom's and grabbed DD. Apparently, everyone had been waiting for me. Mom had already called Jen to see if I hadn't forgotten to pick up DD.

I sped to Lace's. Not that it would matter. I was sure they all had something to say about me being behind schedule. DD ran into the house to greet her cousins as soon as I pulled into the driveway. She didn't even give me a chance to turn the car off. They weren't really cousins, but they called us all "tt' or Auntie, so that made them cousins.

Robbie met me at the door. "Hey, Nika," he said as he went in for an awkward hug. "How are you feeling?" he asked.

"I'm good, thanks for asking," I said as I maneuvered past him into the house. The house smelled delicious. I was so ready to eat. I missed Lace's cooking. She could throw down.

When Lace and Jen got into the kitchen, all bets were off for dieting. I walked into the kitchen and noticed the three of them were one glass away from being two shades in the wind. "Perfect," I thought, "no questions for sure." "Join the party," Sasha yelled as she embraced me tightly.

Jen hugged me and whispered, "It's done." Lace winked and put her glass in the air. I smiled. I was grateful for our friendship.

"Nika, this is Bald Guy," Lace announced as some guy was walking past, kissing her on the cheek.

The said guy then walked up to me and hugged me tightly. "If you have any more problems out of your husband, you let me know. Any firster of Lace's is a firster of mine."

I laughed.

"What's funny?" Bald Guy asked.

"Nothing," I responded. "Thank you, and if needed, I'll take you up on that offer. Bald Guy walked into the garage out of the ear hustling range.

"What the fuck, Lace? You have a random using internal language," I asked. Jen and Sasha looked at me and smiled.

"You don't know the half of it," Jen broadcasted.

"I didn't give him permission. He just heard me use it with you guys on the phone or maybe I used it when I talked about y'all. I don't know how he heard it. He picked it up and started using it on his own. I think he thinks it makes him feel like part of the group," Lace explained.

"Did you tell him this was a girl-only group?" I asked. Lace rolled her eyes and ignored me. Jen, Sasha and I laughed.

I peeked in the garage and saw the DJ setting up. I started helping where I could. Since I was late, Lace had already cooked the dishes I was supposed to make. Just about everything was done. I took a stroll to the patio door and saw Bald Guy putting out three trash cans, placing them deliberately.

"We set up a spot by the lake for a bonfire, too," Jen said as she saw me staring outside. "Just in case anyone wants to sit out there. I imagine that's where the smokers would go," Jen continued. "Wow, they really had thought of everything." I looked over at Jen and nodded. I wanted to ask them questions, but there were too many ears around. I thought I would feel something for Jay, knowing that he was gone for good. But I didn't feel anything but joy. I was not sure if I was happy he was gone, or if I was still on a high from Lamar.

"Hey, babe," Bald Guy said, walking up to Lace, "do you need anything else? I'm going to go shower if you're good."

"Nope, I'm good," Lace said as she kissed him on his lips. I almost choked on the wine I was drinking.

"What the hell, Lace?" I said through my coughs.

"Shut up! I'm going to shower," Lace snarled. Jen and Sasha had already showered and gotten dressed. They were sipping on their wine, laughing at me watching Lace.

"What the hell?" I asked, looking at them both.

"All I know is that she has spent at least the last four days with him," Sasha offered.

"Four whole days?" I asked.

"We don't know for sure. She's being mighty quiet about this random," Jen stated.

People started arriving around five. It was winter, but these folks sure weren't acting like it. The turnout was much bigger than we expected, considering the holiday season had just begun. We purposely set the food up outside on the deck to make sure the yard was utilized.

Lace's random had finished showering. He walked out of her bedroom, dressed in dark jeans and a pullover, smiling way too hard. We couldn't help but take note. He was sexy and just Lace's type. He reminded me a lot of Marcus. "Come to think of it; Lace hasn't even mentioned Marcus again. I know we've been busy, but that's not like Lace. When she wants to know something, she wants to know. Bald Guy must really have her mind distracted. I like him," I thought silently. I usually liked Lace's randoms. Most of them were attentive and funny and always into her way more than she was into them.

"What are you nodding your head at?" Jen asked.

I hadn't noticed I was nodding my head, but I guessed I was. "Have you noticed Lace hasn't mentioned Marcus; you think it has something to do with the random?" I asked.

"Who knows," Jen replied. "She was probably just preoccupied with everything going on."

"The way she cried last Saturday, I can't imagine her not wanting to know," Jen continued.

"Yea, but she hasn't asked," Nika chimed in. Bald Guy was starting the bonfire as we had our conversation. People flocked to the to the flames as we expected.

Tony walked up behind me and whispered something sweet in my ear.

"Hi, honey, I didn't even know you were here. Let me show you around," I responded. Tony laughed and reminded me that he'd seen the place before.

"I know you've seen the house but not the yard or the lake. Let's walk out back," I ordered. Tony complied. We walked outback, showing no affection as the kids were outside playing. The kids were having the time of their lives. Bald Guy was out there leading the kiddie pack. As Tony and I were walking toward the lake, the kids were lining up to play dodge ball. An old school outdoor game. I laughed.

"Someone is going to be crying soon," I said out loud.

"You're right," Tony co-signed.

There were chairs outback by the lake for us to sit, but I had no intention of sitting. The sun was going down, and I wanted to capture the setting. I closed the gate as we walked through and led Tony to the small dock in the lake. It had huge pillars that needed to be replaced or repaired. My money was on replacing them. But, they were perfect for what I needed. I purposely wore a skirt today, just for this moment. Once we reached the dock, I looked back at Tony and pulled my skirt up just above my ass.

He started to laugh. "You're crazy. It's freezing out here," Tony said.

"You won't be cold for long," I promised. Clearly, he believed me. Tony unzipped his pants and yanked his dick out. He moved my panties to the side and fucked me hard. I used the pillar to maintain my balance as his thrust became harder and faster.

"Don't come in me," I whispered.

"Shit," Tony yelled right as he was about to come. He pulled his dick out and released himself out into the wooded area. I purposefully positioned us right where Jay's body fell after Jen shot him.

I stayed in position for a moment, taking in the scenery and particularly taking notes to see if anything was floating in the water. I also looked for any noticeable disturbed areas in the back. I turned and kissed Tony as he fixed himself. He laughed and said, "Girl, I can't believe you just did that with all these people here."

"No one can see us," I assured him. I took another quick glimpse around and noted there was no debris that could point to us.

"You hungry?" I asked.

"Starving," Tony replied.

"Come on; I'll make you a plate," I announced. Tony and I headed back toward the house. The kids were still outside playing, and so was Bald Guy.

"What did you guys do about your friend's husband?" Tony asked.

"We decided to leave it in God's hands. Nika said that Jay wasn't the one that attacked her. We know she's lying, but we can't want revenge more than she wants revenge. So, we're leaving it with God," I responded.

"It's probably a good thing. Karma's a bitch," Tony said. I ignored his comment. "Fuck Karma! Where was Karma when I needed her! Karma don't want no parts of us anyway," I thought silently.

As we got closer to the house, I noticed Lace's previous favorite random walking toward the patio. No doubt, looking for Lace, I was sure. "She never just invites one random." Pasta Guy, what Lace called him, spotted Lace near the kitchen talking to a few of her boat friends, Michelle and Tasha. Apparently, during deployment, she really bonded with those two. I hadn't met them yet, but she did tell us they were coming, and we would love them. "Lace is usually a pretty good judge of character. I'm sure we'll love them as much as she does."

LACE

"Hey, you," Pasta Guy said as he kissed me on my neck. I turned my head as far as I could to make sure it was who I thought it was. I also felt compelled to see if I was in view of Bald Guy. I didn't know why. I never really cared if they all knew about each other.

"It's so good to see you," I said with a huge smile.

"You too," Pasta Guy responded, embracing me tightly.

Pasta Guy and I met while we were stationed in MD. He got stationed here in Norfolk while I was on deployment. I was so excited when he emailed me the news. We've been fucking about three years, taking occasional breaks when one of us was on deployment or back in training. I hadn't seen him since I was in Pensacola before my deployment. He was in training in Biloxi, Mississippi, and invited me over to spend the weekend with him. It was worth the drive. I usually didn't drive to see randoms, but he was my favorite for years. He was not like the others. He didn't pressure me about being in a relationship or any of that shit. He lets me be me, and I let him be him.

I was looking forward to spending some time with Pasta Guy tonight. We normally didn't do any public display of affection, but Pasta Guy was feeling some type of way with his tight embrace. As Pasta Guy released me from his embrace, I felt a hand around my waist. It was Bald Guy; I knew it before I saw him. I felt it in my spirit.

"Hey, sweetie! I've been looking for you," Bald Guy said while turning me to face him. Bald Guy kissed me right in my mouth. It was long and wet, and I couldn't help but participate. I finally freed my lips from Bald Guy and saw Pasta Guy still standing there, watching and waiting.

"Jaxton, this is…." I drew a fucking blank. I could not remember Pasta Guy's name. "Fuck," I screamed in my head.

Pasta Guy searched my face, realizing I had forgotten his name. He reached his hand out to Jaxton, "I'm Cas," Pasta Guy said. I was so embarrassed. Although I knew their real names, I never used them.

"I'm sorry, Cas, I was thrown off a little. I never call you Cas, so, my bad…" I said, trying to recover from my forgetfulness.

"Lace calls me Pasta Guy, but it's reserved for her," Pasta Guy continued.

Bald Guy tightened his grip around my waist. "It was nice to meet you, Cas," Bald Guy said as he motioned me to walk with him down the hall into my bedroom. I completely melted inside. I made eye contact with Jen, looking for an intervention, but she smiled and turned the other way. "Bitch," I thought.

Bald Guy opened the door to my bedroom, walked in, and sat on the bed. He pulled me close to him and positioned me in between his legs. I wasn't sure what was about to happen or what was about to be said, so I stayed silent.

"I'm staying the night, Lace. Let Pasta Guy and all your other little friends out there know," Bald Guy declared. He then stood up, leaned down and kissed me just as passionately as he did in front of Pasta Guy. "They don't have to leave, but they won't be staying," he continued as he smacked my ass on his way out of the bedroom.

I didn't know why that turned me on the way it did. I fell on the bed, laughing. Jen, Sasha and Nika busted in seconds later. "Were you bitches standing there waiting for him to leave?" I asked.

"No, we stood in the living room waiting," Nika replied, laughing.

The rest of the evening was filled with me reconnecting with everyone, eating, and having a great time. I danced a lot, with Bald Guy, of course. I purposely stayed my distance from all other randoms. I didn't care to have one-on-one talks anymore. Plus, I already knew I would be fucking Bald Guy tonight, so it was no need to stir the pot of randoms.

"What time is it?" I asked.

Bald Guy was already in the midst of performing morning glory when I asked. He didn't acknowledge my question and continued his duties until I climaxed. I was still half-sleep but ready and willing to receive what was being offered. Bald Guy climbed on top of me and slid his hard dick inside. We rocked slowly together until we both climaxed. I was not sure what we did that morning, but it surely wasn't fucking. I lay there silently for a few minutes before I mustered up the strength to get out of bed.

After showering, I walked out of my bedroom to a sparkling clean house. "Who cleaned up?" I asked. Nika poked her head up from the sofa, "Michelle and I. We talked all night as we cleaned. We have a lot in common," Nika continued. I smiled. I knew they would hit it off. Michelle and Nika had a lot in common, aside from both being in abusive relationships.

"What time did Michelle leave?" I asked.

"I didn't. I'm still here," Michelle said, not sitting up or moving. I walked over to the living room and saw her lying on the loveseat. I laughed.

"Who else is here?" I asked.

"Jen was here, but she left early to head to work," Nika replied.

I took a peek in the back yard and noticed it too had been cleaned. "Who cleaned the back yard?"

"Me and a few of the other stragglers that were here," Bald Guy replied. I didn't even realize he had followed me out of the room.

"You passed out while the party was in full swing," Bald Guy continued.

"That's normal. Get used to it. She'll leave you hanging at her own events every time," Nika replied. Nika and I both laughed, recognizing the truth in her statement.

"Nika, my flight leaves at 6, we should leave here around 4:30," I stated.

"I'm taking you to the airport," Bald Guy announced.

"Yea! Lace, your boyfriend is taking you to the airport. He informed us last night," Nika responded as she and Michelle giggled like schoolgirls.

CHAPTER 15
NIKA

"A father and son out on a fishing trip discovered a body in the Indian River. The body has not yet been identified, but it is believed to be that of a Sailor that went missing over two weeks ago," the news anchor reported. I turned the volume on the TV down. I didn't want DD to hear. They had been running this story non-stop since yesterday. I was obsessed with hearing them talk about it. I couldn't file for the insurance money until Jay's body had been found and identified. Although I didn't need the money, a part of me felt like it wouldn't be completely over until the claim was paid.

"Mommy, Mommy, do you hear the door?" DD yelled. "Yes, dear, I'll get it," I responded. Truth is I hadn't heard the door. I was busy reading the lips of the news anchor. I turned the TV off and went to answer the door. I looked through the peephole and saw the Navy Chaplin and Military police. They had found my missing husband. He had been shot in the head, and it appeared to be self-inflicted. He was almost unrecognizable. The news came, as we expected. What was unexpected were the tears I shed. I cried hysterically. I'm sure that I was not crying for Jay, though. I was crying over Lamar. I had been for the past few days, silently, of course. This was the first opportunity I had to cry publicly.

My heart was broken. I hadn't spoken to Lamar in two weeks. Since the day we had sex. My calls, texts, and emails had all gone unanswered. My Merry Christmas and Happy New Year texts went unanswered. I was heartbroken and couldn't talk to anyone about it. I was thankful that Jay's body had been found. It gave me a reason to cry openly.

My thoughts had truly been consumed by the loss of Lamar, not the disappearance of my husband. I could give a negative fuck about Jay. I thought about every awakening moment I spent with Lamar. I started to question if any of it was real? There was no way it could have been. Jay's disappearance had been all over the news, yet he hadn't called to check on me. "Could Lamar be just like all the other guys we talked so much shit about?"

I spent the next few days back and forth on base and at the police station. Michelle accompanied me most of the time. She was on house hunting leave as she had officially received her orders back to Norfolk.

Michelle also had no knowledge of what we had done, so it worked out perfectly. She was all our alibies without even knowing it.

Michelle was simply sitting in the police station, waiting for me as she went through all the pictures on her phone, which she had taken at the welcome back party. The detective who had just walked out of the interview room to grab me some water walked by and saw the pictures she was strolling through. The detective asked her a few innocent questions about the date and time of the pictures. She told them all about Lace's welcome home party and all the work we had to do to prepare it. "It was basically a weekend event," Michelle told him. "We started Friday and finished Saturday, and most of us stayed over until Sunday. That was when I met Nika," she continued. "It was a great weekend. We'll invite you next time," she said with a smile. With that information, along with the pictures she involuntarily shared, we were taken off any list the cops thought to put us on.

Although it was an apparent suicide, the cops still had to do their investigations before closing the case. Thanks to Michelle, it was closed quicker than we could have imagined. I was surprised, yet relieved it was all over. But, I still cried. Again, not for Jay, but for Lamar.

"Hey, Nika," Lace said, as I answered the phone.

"Hey, Lace," I answered through sobbing tears.

"I'm just checking on you. Jen and Sasha said you were having a tough time. Is there anything I can do?" Lace asked.

"No, I'm fine, and Michelle has been over a few times, making sure all is good," I informed Lace.

"That's great. I'm glad you two are hitting it off," Lace continued.

"Hey, Nika," someone yelled from the background.

"Who is that?" I asked.

Lace continued holding the conversation as if she didn't hear my question.

"Sorry to hear about your husband," the voice yelled again.

"Lace, who the fuck is that?"

"It's Jaxton," Lace said with a sigh.

"Bald Guy?" I asked.

"Yes, if you must know," Lace replied while rolling her eyes, I'm sure.

"He flew down to spend the holidays with me and help me drive back. That's all," Lace concluded.

"What? Did he meet your mom and T?" I asked with excitement.

"Got to go, Nika, I'll talk to you later," Lace said as she dismissed my call.

A part of me was happy for Lace. I like Bald Guy. We all did. We liked how Lace responded to him. She didn't dismiss him or treat him how she normally treated other randoms. When he spoke, she listened. She didn't go back and forth with him. When he decided on something, and it made sense, she agreed. Although they were simple and meaningless decisions, she still didn't debate him. That was exactly what Lace needed.

That was what Lamar was for me. He was a decision-maker. He was my go-to for everything. He was my mentor and coach, guiding me through all the tough situations in life. I compared every man to Lamar. He was the epitome of what a man should be, in my eyes at least. He made my life better. Maybe I should start using past tense for anything that pertained to Lamar. He hadn't been my life mentor or coach since I slept with him. Maybe I pushed him too far too fast.

LACE

Simba picked me up from the airport as planned. Although we lived in different states, my mother's one request was that we always made it home for New Years. Most years, it worked out that way. This year we would all be home for both Christmas and New Year. Mom was over the moon, thrilled.

"How was your flight?" Simba asked when he picked me up. "It was fine. Where's T?" I asked
"He didn't want to ride," Simba informed me. My feelings were crushed. "I've been gone for almost a year, and he didn't want to see his mommy," I thought silently. In the midst of my thoughts, out pooped T from the third row.
"I'm here, Mom. I got you, welcome home," he yelled with excitement. I missed my son. I wanted to hold him in the front seat with me on the ride to my mom's. Instead, I opted to sit in the back seat with him. T talked the whole ride home. Clearly, he had a lot to tell me. A lot had happened in kindergarten, and he wanted to fill me in on all of it.

We arrived at mom's house, and she greeted me with open arms at the door. She was so excited. Yanni and Nathan were both already home. I was the last to arrive. I hadn't seen Yanni in four or maybe five years. She hadn't come home at mom's request. She looked good. She was well. Of course, I spoke to Nathan every chance I got while on deployment. I brought each of them back something from my journey. They were all so thankful. We spent a few hours talking about my trip, the things I loved; the things I hated; the cities we must visit as a family and the ones we should visit with friends. It was good catching up with my siblings.

Mom abruptly switched gears to discuss her annual fish fry and all the duties she had planned for us. "By the way, Lace, you have a delivery. It's in the kitchen on the table," Mom said. I walked into the kitchen and saw a beautiful banquet of red roses.

"I don't see anything but some flowers, Mom," I yelled out.

"That's it, Lace. They're for you," Mom responded. I searched for the card. I found it hidden within and not on the cardholder where it should be. A clear indication that Mom had already opened and read it. "I miss you already, Jaxton," the card read. I smiled. I wanted to laugh out loud, but I smiled instead.

"He's so full of it. He literally just met me. He can't miss me yet," I thought.

"I got the flowers you sent," I said as Jaxton answered the phone.

"I want to be with you for the New Year. I don't want to spend it without you. Plus, I've never been to Miami. I think it will be fun," Jaxton blurted all without taking a breath.

I laughed. "You can't be serious. Tickets will be stupid high, and you'll have to get a hotel, and I know they're all booked. My mom won't allow you to stay here," I said.

"I completely understand. I'm not worried about any of that. If it's cool, I'll come down tomorrow. I'll help you drive back," he announced.

"If you come down tomorrow, you will be here for Christmas and the New Year. Don't you have a family to spend time with?" I asked.

"Does tomorrow work for you?" he asked again.

"Sure," I responded indifferently.

I thought Jaxton was blowing smoke up my ass until I received an email with his flight itinerary attached. I wasn't ready for him to meet my son or my family. "Why did I agree to this shit?" I thought. The next day, I picked Jaxton up from Ft Lauderdale airport and laid down all the dos and don'ts. "No public display of affection. We are friends only. You wanted to come to Miami because you had never been, not because of me! Understand?" I said sternly.

Jaxton smiled and gave me a sarcastic salute, "Ma'am, yes, ma'am!" he responded.

We pulled into my mom's driveway. I put the truck in park right as Jaxton leaned over and kissed me. My insides became warm. A feeling I hadn't felt in a long time. Jaxton jumped out of the truck, walked over to the driver's side and grabbed my hand as I got out of the truck and walked into the house as if he belonged there. I introduced him to everyone, and he announced he was my boyfriend. I laughed so hard. "What happened to what I said in the truck?" I asked through my laughter.

"I knew you wanted them to all know the truth," he said, smiling.

"I didn't even know the damn truth. Next time, fill me in first," I demanded. I wasn't ready for a boyfriend or a monogamist relationship, but it was the holidays. I played along.

My mom adored Jaxton. She was more besotted than I was. The entire family liked him, even Yanni, and she didn't like anyone. T took a strong likeness to Jaxton as well. I think that was by Jaxton's design. He knew if T liked him, he'd probably have a better chance of sticking around. The next week and a half, with Jaxton and my family, were great. I played tour guide and took Jaxton to all the best places to go in Miami, which was never where the tourist went. We hung out all day, and I spent most nights with him. Bringing in 2005 with Jaxton was great. It was one of my best NYEs to date. On the drive back to Norfolk, the truck was filled with the sound of our voices the entire ride. I got to know a lot more about Jaxton, and I realized I liked him a lot.

JEN

"Ma, Ma," Alisha yelled, tugging me out of my thoughts.
I reached down and picked up my princess. "Yes, sweetheart, how can Mommy help you?" I asked.
"I want breakfast, please," she replied innocently.
"Sure, sweetheart. Go and ask Daddy if he would also like breakfast." Alisha ran off to wake her father.
I knew it would take some time, so I walked out to the patio and lit a cigarette. I stood there thinking about all we had done the previous year, praying that next year would be better; praying that we would be better; praying that we would make better choices with men and praying that there would be no need for us to go to extremes to protect one another.

"Mommy!" I heard Alisha yell from inside the house. I threw away my cigarette and ran inside. There were cops everywhere with guns drawn. Alisha was yelling and screaming. She was terrified. I ran to her and held her tightly. "We have a warrant for your arrest and a warrant to search your place," I heard one of the cops say. I felt like I was on an episode of Law and Order. I wasn't sure if it was the Special Victims Unit, or the original series. It was an out of body experience. I had those often.

The cops searched every inch of my house. The last thing they searched was the trash cans. They found all the bags that contained the tape, rag, and zip ties we took off Jay before he went into the lake. The tape had his hair and DNA all over it. I was supposed to take all the bags to work the day after Lace's party and put them in the incinerator, but I forgot and simply put them in the trash cans in my house. I figured it would be just the same.

"How would they have known to search my house?" I wondered. They yanked Alisha out of my arms and handcuffed me while my daughter stood there, hollering and screaming. Robbie finally came out of the bedroom in his PJs. He reached for Alisha and stood up with the biggest smile on his face. "This bastard is smiling. It was Robbie," I thought immediately. "Would he really call the cops on me? He must have. It was him, dammit." I was convinced.

"I told you to stop hanging with those girls, Jen. They're bad news," Robbie said while still smiling.

I jumped up from the nightmare in a cold sweat. It was day 12 that I had the same exact dream. The dreams were so vivid. They felt so real. I woke up and checked all the garbage cans again. I knew I put all the bags in the incinerator, but every time I had the nightmare, I double, and triple checked again.

SASHA

"Another one down," I whispered silently to myself. We had been sitting on pins and needles for weeks now. I felt like we could finally breathe. We had gotten away with it again. It took the investigation team no time to rule Jay's death a suicide. We were overly excited. Nika started the process to claim Jay's Servicemembers' Group Life Insurance. Unlike regular insurance, this insurance still paid out in the cases of suicide. Lace, Nika and Jen weren't sure, but that was one of the few things I remembered from being a personnel man. If you were covered during the time of death, your beneficiaries still received their payout, regardless of how you died. I had seen my fair chair of suicides in the Navy. Sadly, it was quite common, almost routine.

I also knew they didn't investigate suicides in the Navy as they did in the civilian world. Jay had Nika's rape case lingering over him. It was easy for the authorities to see why he would kill himself. Death or prison, Jay wasn't the type to take instructions. No way would he have made it in prison, especially not for rape.

We were stoked, and I wanted to celebrate. Jay had left Nika with one final parting gift. She was due in October. She was still in her first trimester, sick as shit and hating life. She contemplated aborting it, but she had always wanted another child, so she decided to keep it. We were all very surprised yet supportive. We loved kids. Although, we thought we were finished having them by now. Wishful thinking, I guessed. We were still very young. We hadn't even reached 30 yet.

I wanted to go out and celebrate! I called up Michelle, but she was keeping Nika company, and Nika needed the company more than I did. Lace was watching Alisha. Jen had just started her new job at Norfolk General on the weekend shift. It was the worst possible shift ever, but it did get her out of the nursing home, and away from all those memories of Axel. Not that having the kids would stop Lace from parting, but she was also booed up with her new boo thang, Jaxton. I didn't care what she said; she was in love. She didn't believe you could fall in love that fast, but the rest of us knew you could, and Lace was living proof of it happening. Every time someone mentioned his name, she would smile ear to ear. Jaxton did everything for Lace and showered her with attention. He loved T too. They had a great relationship. Jaxton would take T out every Saturday, just the two of them to bond. T had a lot of respect for Jaxton, as we all did.

Carter had just taken a one-year assignment to Afghanistan. We were still officially married, but by the time he got back, we'd be divorced. The kids and I would be in our new home. I thought about buying a house in Chesapeake, near Lace. It was an established, older community, and all the neighbors treated you like family. I loved that. I was finally becoming happy. Last year was hard, but we planned to make this year much better.

I called Tony up and told him I was going to club Rain and demanded he meet me there. Of course, he agreed. Then I phoned one of the girls that worked the boutique with me. She was mad hype to hang out. She absolutely had a girl crush on me. Jen joked about it all the time. I got all dolled up. I pulled half of my hair up into a messy bun on top of my head and left the back out to flow freely. I wore a black sleeveless and deep cut backless dress. I got it from the boutique. The owners wanted $150 for the dress. I swiped a new one out of the box and kept it moving. The way it looked on me, it was worth the $150. I couldn't wait to see Tony. Since Carter had been gone, Tony had been spending the night here and there, but this week, he opted to stay home, since Valentine's Day was during the week. I wanted to show him what he was missing.

"Lace, I'm dropping the kids off with you on the way to the club. Do you have gas in the truck? I'm out and don't feel like stopping," I announced without taking a breath when Lace answered the phone.
"I'll be here, and yes, there is gas in my truck," Lace responded.
"OK, see you in a bit." I packed a bag for the kids and loaded them into the car. I cranked the music all the way up and headed for Lace's. If no one else wanted to celebrate, I would celebrate for all of us.

CHAPTER 16
LACE

I flickered my eyes to Jaxton shaking me, demanding that I wake up. The look on his face was frightening. "The cops are at the door. They need to speak with you," Jaxton continued.

"What time is it?" I asked. "It's almost 6:00 a.m. Lace, get up. Come to the door," Jaxton continued.

I got out of the bed and put on my robe. I purposely didn't put on any clothes just in case I was getting arrested. I wanted the opportunity to come back to my room and get dressed. I didn't know why. It really wouldn't matter at that point.

"Ma'am, there's been an accident. The vehicle is registered to you. Do you know who was driving?" the cop asked.

"Yes, Sasha. Sasha has my truck. She was driving. Is it bad? Where is she?" I asked.

"If you can get to the hospital, you should…" the officer stated. "She's at Norfolk general," he replied. "Do you need a ride?" he asked.

"No, officer, my car is here," Jaxton chimed in. I stood there, looking and feeling dazed. I was confused. I didn't know what was happening.

"Go, Lace, go see what's going on," Jaxton instructed.

"The kids are here," I said.

"I have them, just go," Jaxton replied. I raced to the bedroom and threw on whatever I could find and grabbed my cellphone and purse and rushed out the door.

Racing through the streets with knots in my stomach as I drove, I called Nika. "Something's happened to Sasha. I don't know how bad it is. I was just told to get to the hospital if I could. You should come too," I said as I arrived in the ER waiting room, frantic.

"I'm here to see my friend, Sasha James," I announced.

"Ma'am, she's still in surgery. Is there someone you would like to call?" the nurse asked.

"Who the fuck do I need to call? How bad is it?" I asked. The young lady didn't answer. She just pitied me. "Yes, yes, can I call Jen Adams? She's a nurse here," I finally asked

I heard them page Jen on the loudspeaker. A few minutes later, I heard the nurse speaking. "Ma'am, nurse Adams is on the line for you."

"Jen," I said through tears. "Something happened to Sasha!" I announced frantically.

"What happened?" Jen asked.

"I don't know; they won't tell me. She's in surgery, here. I'm in the ER waiting room," I responded.

"I'll be right over," Jen said as she hung up.

Nika and Michelle arrived shortly after I spoke with Jen. The same cop that was at my house appeared from nowhere. "Ms. Miles, have you called Ms. James' next of kin.

"Why the fuck would I call her next of kin? What the fuck is going on?" I yelled. I looked over at Nika and Michelle, and they were in full-blown tears. I felt like everyone knew what was happening except me. I grabbed my cellphone and fumbled through the numbers. I began crying hysterically. They wouldn't tell us shit.

"Mom, Mom," I yelled into the phone. "Something happened to Sasha. Can you pray with us?"

"Lace, calm down. I can't understand what you're saying," my mother responded. I always called my mom when things got too tough. She would usually pray me out of whatever I got myself into.

"Can you pray with us, please? Something has happened to Sasha," I said again. My mother began to pray for our healing and strength. Her prayer was eerie. She prayed for our understanding as we go through this tragedy and the loss of our friend.

"What are you talking about, Mom? She's not dead," I shouted. My mother didn't respond. She continued to pray and Nika, Michelle and I began to cry harder than we already were as we listened to my mother's prayer. She prayed as if she had been given the news, which no one else had. She prayed like it was the end. Her prayer angered me.

There was an announcement being made. Codes being yelled, and all sorts of movements happening as my mother finished her pray. Jen appeared from a hallway with four doctors and a priest. She was practically being carried out by two other nurses. They ushered us into a room. Sonya had just arrived. I called her right before I called my mother. The vibe in the room was unnerving. Jen had latched onto me, Nika and Michelle and wouldn't let go.

We sat in a windowless room with a glass soundproof door, all seated, while the doctors explained that Sasha was two miles from her house when she passed out and lost control of the vehicle. She was ejected from the roof of a Dodge Durango and lodged between a hole in the roof. Emergency rescuers tried to save her. "By the time she arrived at the hospital, she had suffered a great deal and lost a lot of blood. We did everything we could to save her," one of the doctors said.

"We did all we could," the youngest female doctor said through tears. Sasha's time of death was 8:34 a.m., 19 February 2005.

"NO! NO! NO!" I screamed as I fell to the floor.

JEN

I saw Lace fall, through the tears in my eyes, but I couldn't help her up. I couldn't move. I was not even sure I was breathing. I just sat there and cried. It was like we were robots for the next few minutes. I didn't think the doctors even gave us time to process the news we had just heard. The doctors immediately announced that Sasha was an organ donor. Her body was still warm, and they needed permission to extract her organs. Sonya was on the phone with her parents. You could hear her mom screaming through the phone. Sonya's parents asked her to sign off on Sasha's organ donation forms, but she was a wreck and unable to do so. Sonya passed that task to Lace.

Lace couldn't come to grips with the news we had just received. Lace and Sasha were like sisters, especially after that thing with Sonya. Lace didn't have a relationship with Yani, so we were the only sisters she had. Lace was doing fine with the organ donation conversation until they asked about the skin on Sasha's eyelids. I think, at that point, it hit her just how real it was, and she couldn't continue.

I had been on both ends of this conversation. I knew the difficulties of being asked the questions from the patients' perspective as I had sat with many patients during this time. I also knew the importance of asking the questions, though simple in nature, some of the tiniest pieces of someone else could be life-changing for others. I had never personally experienced it with someone this close to me. It felt different. Sasha was a sister to all of us.

I don't know how long we stayed there. I feel like we didn't get back to Lace's until nightfall. All the kids were there except DD. Nika had dropped her at her Ms. Rodgers on the way to the hospital. Nika left the hospital a few minutes before us to go pick up DD. It was a time when we just needed to hold our babies. She arrived at Lace's not too long behind us.

Jaxton had been with the kids all day. We all walked in and said nothing. Jaxton grabbed Lace. "What happened?" he asked.

Lace didn't respond. She cried into his shirt, silently so the kids wouldn't hear. I gathered the kids in the living room. Lace released Jaxton.

We all held the kids close. Interlocking our fingers, we sat with them in the middle. We didn't say anything. We just all sat there. Lace, Nika, Michelle and I cried and allowed silent tears to fall. We never mentioned anything to the kids.

NIKA

We all stayed the night at Lace's. We couldn't bear to part from one another. We tried holding the kids as long as possible, but they didn't sit still. They had no desire to be near us. The four of us slept in the living room. Jaxton stayed over too. He continued watching the kids and us. He was so attentive to us. I was thankful he stayed.

Sonya arrived at Lace's house the next morning to pick up Sasha's kids. Their parents had arrived and went straight to the hospital to see Sasha. Jen went to see Sasha after the doctors gave us the news yesterday. She said Sasha was bloated. She looked nothing like herself. Her hair was blood-soaked and stuck to her face. I was glad I opted not to see Sasha. I didn't want that to be the last memory of my friend.

I held Sasha's boys close and tight. I didn't want to let them go. A part of me knew that I would never see them again if I did, but I needed to see them. That was the only way Sasha would remain in our lives. Sonya practically had to pry them from me. Neither Lace nor Jen bothered hugging them. They thought they would break down if they did, and the children didn't know about their mother yet. We hadn't told them about Sasha. Her parents asked us not to.

Funeral arrangements were made quickly. Sasha's body was flown from Norfolk to Dothan, where she would be buried in her family's plot. Carter flew from Afghanistan straight to Dothan as well. Jen, Lace, Jaxton and I took leave to attend the funeral. Michelle stayed in Norfolk and watched the children for us.

We flew into Atlanta the day of the funeral. Lace's mom flew up from Miami and met us in ATL. She never allowed Lace to go through life-changing events without her. We rented an SUV for the drive down to Dothan. Mrs. Miles prayed before we started the ride down and slept the rest of the way. It was the longest car ride I ever had to endure. Jaxton drove while he held Lace's hand in the front seat. He kissed it periodically, consoling her. "I think he's in love with her," I whispered to Jen.

"One of them is in love for sure," Jen said. We both laughed. Lace heard us but ignored us as usual. It was nice to see Lace with someone other than a random. She still wasn't ready to admit that they were an item, but it didn't matter. We all knew, even if she didn't.

I wrote a poem for Sasha. We rehearsed it on the way down as we were asked to recite it at the funeral. I didn't know how we planned on doing that. We could barely mention her name without tears flowing. I had cried so much over the past few weeks. I was hoping my tear ducks dried up and withered away.

I was pretty sure I was done crying for Jay and Lamar. I still hadn't heard from Lamar. I knew he must have heard about Sasha by now and still hadn't even attempted to call me. The thought of that made me angry with him. I had never been angry at Lamar, but I was now. I tried hard not to think about him. It was becoming easier with everything happening around me.

We arrived at Sasha's parents' house with a few minutes to spare before the procession. We got out of the car and greeted the family. Sasha's boys ran straight to us, holding on tightly. I missed their little faces. We greeted Carter while Sonya stood uncomfortably close to him. We greeted her, as well. It was a surreal feeling being in my friend's hometown without my friend. "I don't even understand why she's being buried here. She hated it here."

"Nika, is that your work friend?" Lace asked, using stupid air quotes. "What was his name again? Did he know Sasha?" she continued.

I looked to my right and saw Lamar walking toward us. He was in no rush. He walked slow but determined. I ran to him. He opened his arms, and I fell into him and cried.

"Where have you been, asshole?" I asked. I would normally never talk to Lamar like that, but my emotions were all over the place. He ignored me and held me tightly.

"I'm here now," he responded softly.

Lamar rode with us to the funeral. He sat next to me during the service, holding and consoling me. I was thankful he was there until he leaned over and whispered in my ear, "I was at your apartment the morning your friends took Jay. I followed them to Lace's. I struggled with staying silent or going to the cops, but once I heard about Sasha, I figured Karma had already given you girls your life sentence. Your secret is safe with me!" he concluded, as he kissed my forehead.

LACE

I didn't even hear them call our names up to speak. My mother nudged me on my right side. Nika and Jen had already walked into the aisle. Jaxton had also moved to allow me to pass. All this movement went on without me noticing a thing. We walked up front, arms interlocked with one another. We stood so close to the casket. I was grateful it was a closed casket. Sasha's parents didn't want anyone to see her in the state in which they saw her in. Sasha would have wanted it closed too. She always wanted to look her best, and from what I was told, she was far from it.

I started the poem off, but I doubt anyone understood a word I was saying, my cries became uncontrollable. Jen was holding me as tight as she could, but her and Nika's cries were just as bad. I looked out to the sea of people that came to say goodbye to my friend. She was loved beyond words.

People flew from all over to pay their respects to Sasha. I couldn't make out any faces. I was trying to focus on my mother just to get through the poem, but it was useless. My heart was broken, and my pain was on display for everyone to see. At some point, I was not sure if we even finished the poem, Lamar and Jaxton came upfront to usher us back. I was a mess. Jen sat next to my mother, and my mother consoled her, while Jaxton consoled me.

As if the service wasn't draining enough, we still had to attend the burial. I was completely emotionally spent. When they lowered Sasha's coffin into the ground, I felt my heart drop. I literally buckled over in agony

I lost my dad a few years back, but I was pregnant at the time and wasn't allowed to grieve. I remember my aunts robbing my back, telling me that I needed to be strong for the baby. I had to remember not to stress the baby. It was a game of mind-fucking. I thought it was the worst feeling in the world, being asked not to grieve or cry for your father to protect your unborn child. I was wrong.

I would have welcomed having a reason to be strong now. But I didn't, and I cried uncontrollably. Jaxton was finally able to calm me as we walked back to the car. I had no desire to go back to Sasha's parents' house, but according to my mom, "We had to, it was the right thing to do."

"Lace," I heard a familiar voice scream as we walked back to the truck. I knew the voice, but I couldn't place it now. I turned slowly and stared into the face of Marcus as he ran toward us. Marcus, in the flesh after all this time. I had no more tears left. Marcus caught up to Jen, Nika and Lamar first as they walked slightly behind Jaxton and me. Marcus hugged Jen, tightly and kissed her on the cheek. Then turned to Nika and displayed the same affection and offered his condolences for Jay. "He knows Jay too," I thought as I saw some movement. I believed Lamar was introduced. I saw a handshake, but I was taken aback. I wasn't sure what was happening, standing there in shock. Looking ridiculous, I'm sure. Jaxton still stood next to me, holding me tightly. My mother had already gotten in the truck.

Marcus walked a few more feet and came in for a hug. His embrace was as I remembered it. I didn't hug him back. The fire inside me began to burn. I jerked out of his embrace in anger. Jaxton put his arm around my waist to calm me as if he knew I was about to explode. "Hi, I'm Jaxton," he said, reaching out his hand. Marcus extended his hand, as well.

"I'm Marcus. Nice to meet you," Marcus responded.

"Lace, can I talk to you, alone?" Marcus asked.

"What are you doing here? How do you know Sasha, Nika and Jen?" I attempted to shout, but my voice failed me and began to crack.

"Carter and I have been friends for years. Naturally, I would be here to support him. Do you think we can talk?" Marcus continued.

The blood inside of me began to boil. "For years? How many years?" I asked. I looked over to Jen and Nika and became furious at the sight of them. They both watched me intently. Marcus did not answer me. Instead, he waited for a response to his questions. "I don't think that's a good idea!" I snarled.

"Just for a few minutes!" Marcus begged.

"Maybe another day," I suggested.

"When you're ready, give me a call, Jen and Nika both have my number," Marcus concluded as he turned and walked away.

EPILOGUE
MICHELLE

As I walked out of the courthouse, I could literally feel the weight floating off my shoulders. It was as if my life was starting over. I was born again. The sun was shining bright, and the air was crisp, or maybe it wasn't, but that was how I saw things. Everything was clear, and I was focused!

I got nothing material in the divorce: no car, and no place to stay, no money, but that was fine by me. He could have it all. I just wanted out of that marriage with my life and my two girls.

It was still early. I figured I had time to make it to the Personnel Support Department (PSD). With divorce papers in hand, the one thing I wanted was my maiden name, and I didn't want to waste any time getting it back. I had the information desk at the courthouse call me a taxi to take me onto the base since he took my cell phone too.

The taxi arrived after a short fifteen-minute wait. It dropped me at the gate of Norfolk Naval Station, and I walked the rest of the way. The buildings don't seem so far when you drive. I arrived at PSD, hot and sweaty, but happy and smiling. I signed the log to be seen and sat and waited my turn patiently with the rest of the hopeful name changing sailors. I was on cloud nine. I was so happy and at peace. I didn't notice anyone around me until I saw Sonya. She walked out of the service area, smiling. She too was happy, and it showed. I had only met her once a few months ago. It was the day after Sasha died, but I remembered her.

She looked different, though it was something about her. She was glowing. When I finally moved my attention from her face, I noticed she wore a maternity uniform and the name on her uniform shirt read James.

I didn't know Sasha as well as Lace, Nika and Jen, but I did know her well enough to know that her married name had been James. *Why the fuck is Sonya now wearing the name James on her uniform?*